Fun and Games at Malory Towers

P9-APD-298

Malory Towers

Enid Blyton

Enid Blyton

Fun and Games at Malory Towers

Written by Pamela Cox

Based on characters and stories created by Enid Blyton

EGMONT

EGMONT

We bring stories to life

Fun and Games at Malory Towers first published in Great Britain 2009
This edition published in 2013 by Egmont UK Limited
The Yellow Building, 1 Nicholas Road
London, W11 4AN

Distributed by Penguin Books India,
11 Community Centre, Panchsheel Park
New Delhi 110 017 by arrangement with Egmont UK Ltd

Text & Illustrations copyright © Hodder & Stoughton 2013
Written by Pamela Cox

ENID BLYTON ® Copyright © Hodder & Stoughton 2013

ISBN 978 1 4052 7004 5

56891/1

A CIP catalogue record for this title is available from the British Library

Printed and bound in India

This copy is only available in India, Bangladesh, Sri Lanka, Bhutan and Nepal

Stay safe online. Any website addresses listed in this book/magazine are correct at the
time of going to print. However, Egmont is not responsible for content hosted by third
parties. Please be aware that online content can be subject to change and websites can
contain content that is unsuitable for children. We advise that all children are supervised
when using the internet.

EGMONT LUCKY COIN

Our story began over a century ago, when seventeen-year-old
Egmont Harald Petersen found a coin in the street.

He was on his way to buy a flyswatter, a small hand-operated
printing machine that he then set up in his tiny apartment.

The coin brought him such good luck that today Egmont has
offices in over 30 countries around the world. And that lucky
coin is still kept at the company's head offices in Denmark.

Contents

Contents

New girls at Malory Towers

'Isn't it marvellous to be going back to Malory Towers?' said Felicity Rivers excitedly, to her friend Susan Blake. 'And to think we'll be going up into the fifth form! Haven't the years just flown by?'

'Yes,' agreed Susan. 'Sometimes it seems like only yesterday that we were starting out as first formers.'

Felicity had been staying with Susan for a few days, and now Mrs Blake was driving them back to school. First, though, they had to stop to collect a new girl, who was also going to be in the fifth form, on the way.

'Mother, what did you say the new girl was called?' asked Susan.

'Millicent Moon,' answered Mrs Blake. 'I met her mother when I went out to tea the other day, and she seemed very pleasant indeed.'

'Yes, but what is Millicent like?' asked Susan impatiently.

'Well, I don't know, dear, for I didn't meet her,' said Mrs Blake. 'She wasn't there. The family have been living in France for the last year, you know, and Millicent was studying at a music academy there.'

'I wonder if she will be as eccentric as my sister

Darrell's friend, Irene?' said Felicity, with a grin. 'Remember her, Susan?'

'Yes, she was great fun,' said Susan. 'A simply brilliant musician, but completely absent-minded when it came to normal, everyday matters. I say, won't it be marvellous for us if Millicent turns out to be as mad as Irene?'

But when Mrs Blake presently stopped the car outside a neat house, the girl who stepped out didn't look at all mad or eccentric. And she didn't look as if she would be much fun either, thought Felicity and Susan, feeling a little disappointed.

Millicent Moon was tall and slim, with long, straight dark hair, intense dark eyes and a pale, serious face. Her mother and father walked to the car with her, Mr Moon bringing Millicent's trunk with him, and Mrs Blake stepped out of the car to greet them. The three grown-ups chatted for a few moments, while Millicent stood aside, an aloof expression on her face.

Inside the car, Felicity said to Susan, 'She looks awfully serious.'

'Perhaps she is just nervous,' said Susan. 'It must be hard changing schools in the fifth form, when most of the others have known one another for years, and all have their own friends.'

'Yes,' agreed Felicity. 'We must do everything we can to make Millicent feel at home.'

So, when the new girl's trunk was stowed safely in the boot, and Millicent herself slipped into the back of the car beside Felicity and Susan, she received a warm welcome.

'Hallo, Millicent,' said Susan, with a broad smile. 'Nice to meet you. I'm Susan, and this is my friend, Felicity.'

Felicity greeted the girl too, and said, 'I hope you're going to like it at Malory Towers. If there is anything you want to know, just ask Susan and me.'

Millicent gave a little smile, and, as Mrs Blake started the car, said, 'Thank you. I'm sure that I shall be happy, as long as I can play my music, and keep up with my lessons. Music is my life, you see.'

Felicity and Susan looked rather startled at this, for Millicent sounded so very dramatic, and Susan said, 'There are several girls in our form who take music lessons, but none of them are what you could call great musicians. I must say, it will be jolly nice to have someone in the form who can bash out a few tunes on the piano in the common-room, when we feel like having a dance.'

Now it was Millicent's turn to look startled, and Felicity said, 'Perhaps Millicent doesn't play the piano.'

'Oh, I do,' said Millicent coolly. 'And the violin. And the harp. And the flute. But I am used to playing classical music, and not dance tunes.'

Then Millicent turned her head to look out of the window and fell silent, while Felicity and Susan pulled wry faces at one another.

As Millicent evidently wasn't in the mood for conversation, the other two girls began to talk about their friends at Malory Towers, Susan saying, 'Sylvia won't be coming back this term. Her people are moving to Scotland, and she is going to day school there.'

'I shall miss old Sylvia,' said Felicity, with a sigh. 'I didn't much care for her at first, but she turned out to be quite a good sort.'

'I could do with a nice easy time, this term,' said Susan. 'We all worked so hard at passing School Cert in the fourth that I think we deserve a good rest.'

'Did everyone in your form pass, dear?' asked Susan's mother.

'Yes, everyone,' answered Susan. 'Even Nora and Amy, who were both quite certain that they would fail.'

'June sailed through, of course,' said Felicity, a touch of envy in her tone. 'She hardly did any studying at all, yet she still managed to get excellent marks.'

'Typical of June!' laughed Susan. 'I say, she will have to settle down a bit now that she is a fifth former, won't she?'

'Yes, I think it's going to be harder for June than for any of us,' said Felicity, thoughtfully. 'She's so fond of playing jokes and tricks, but that kind of thing is quite out of the question when one becomes a fifth former.'

Susan was about to reply to this when suddenly a low, tuneful humming filled the car. Felicity and Susan looked at one another, startled, as they wondered what it could be, then they realised that it was coming from Millicent. The girl had her eyes closed and her head back as she hummed, then, just as suddenly as it had started, the sound stopped, and Millicent opened her eyes and began rummaging in her schoolbag.

She realised that the others were staring at her, and gave a laugh.

'Sorry,' she said. 'It's just that a new tune has come to me, and I must write it down at once, while it's fresh in my mind.'

She pulled a pen and notebook from her bag, and began jotting down a series of musical notes, while Felicity and Susan watched, fascinated.

'There!' she said at last, in satisfaction. 'I shall try that out later. You did say that there was a piano in the common-room, didn't you?'

'Well, the old fifth formers had one,' said Felicity. 'So it should still be there, unless Miss Grayling has had it moved.'

'Good,' said Millicent. 'Now, do tell me more about Malory Towers.'

Now that she had written down her new tune, Millicent seemed much more amicable, and chatted pleasantly with Felicity and Susan throughout the rest of the journey.

It was a very long drive indeed, and at twelve o'clock Mrs Blake stopped the car and took the girls for lunch at a restaurant. Afterwards, the three of them all felt rather sleepy, and conversation in the car tailed off as both Millicent and Susan closed their eyes. Felicity remained awake, though, for although she felt tired, she was excited too. It was so marvellous to be going back to her beloved Malory Towers, and she simply couldn't wait to see all the others again.

Scatter-brained Nora, and her friend, the placid, good-natured Pam. Then there were Julie and Lucy, who always brought their horses, Jack and Sandy, back to school with them. Not forgetting Amy, Bonnie, Freddie – and June, of course! Who could forget June, with her bold, mischievous ways? Perhaps there would be other new girls, too, thought Felicity, as the car went on its way, getting closer and closer to Malory Towers. What fun that would be!

When they were almost there, Susan woke up, rubbing her eyes before she turned to grin at Felicity.

'Almost there!' she said excitedly.

Then Millicent stirred, and sat up, yawning.

'We're nearly there, Millicent,' said Felicity excitedly. 'Once we turn this corner you will be able to see Malory Towers. Look, there it is! Up on the cliff-top.'

'Heavens, it looks like a castle!' exclaimed Millicent, looking up at the big building, with its four towers. 'How magnificent. I feel sure that I shall be inspired to write some marvellous music in such a setting.'

Millicent had gone all intense again, and Felicity and Susan exchanged glances, trying not to laugh, while Mrs Blake frowned at them in the driving mirror.

At last the car came to a halt in the driveway, and the three girls looked out to see dozens of girls, all chattering away together, greeting friends and saying goodbye to parents.

Felicity could see Nora and Pam in the distance, and she longed to leap out of the car and run across to them.

But she was a sober, serious fifth former now, so she got out of the car in a dignified manner, and waited patiently with Susan and Millicent while Mrs Blake opened the boot and got their things out.

'Do have a good term, all of you,' said Mrs Blake, giving Susan a hug. 'And I shall see you at half-term, dear.'

Then the three girls made their way across the lawn, and found that Pam and Nora had been joined by June and Freddie.

'Hallo there! Had good hols?'

'My goodness, isn't it grand to be back?'

'I can't believe that we are fifth formers now!'

'And who's this? A new girl?'

'Oh yes, this is Millicent Moon,' said Felicity. 'Millicent, meet Pam, Nora, June and Freddie.'

The others greeted the new girl with interest, then Susan said, 'There's something different about you this term, June.'

'Is there?' said June, looking rather startled. 'I can't think what.'

'I know what it is!' cried Susan. 'You have an air of dignity about you.'

'Yes,' agreed Felicity, her eyes twinkling. 'You look far more serious and responsible than you did last term. Like a proper fifth former!'

'I was just thinking that myself,' said Nora, joining in the fun. 'I say, June, perhaps Miss James will make you head of the form now that you've gone all serious and grown-up.'

June gave a snort and said, 'Serious and grown-up? Me? What nonsense! As for Miss James making me head of the form, why, she's more likely to choose Bonnie or Amy!'

The others laughed at the thought of little Bonnie, or the haughty Amy, becoming head-girl, and Nora said, 'I wonder who she will choose? Not me, that's for sure.'

'Well, we will find out tomorrow,' said Pam. 'I say, who's that over there? Another new girl?'

The others looked, and saw a plump, fair girl, with round, grey eyes and a rather bewildered expression, standing alone.

'Poor thing,' said Freddie. 'She looks rather lost. Shall we go and say hallo?'

So the group of fifth formers went across to the new girl and Felicity said, 'Hallo there. You're new, aren't you? What form are you in?'

'I'm in the fifth form, North Tower,' answered the girl, smiling shyly. 'My name's Delia Norris. Are you all fifth formers too?'

'Yes,' answered Susan. 'And we are all in North Tower, so you had better come along with us to Matron.'

Delia bent to pick up her night case, and as she did so it flew open, her belongings spilling out everywhere.

'Oh my gosh!' said Delia, bending down to cram them in again higgledy-piggledy. 'How silly of me. My aunt is always telling me how careless and clumsy I am.'

'Well, that's not very kind of her,' said the outspoken June, and Felicity gave her a nudge, before stooping to help the new girl collect her scattered things.

'Well, my aunt isn't very kind, sometimes,' said Delia, turning red. 'She was awfully glad when my grand-mother decided to pay the fees for me to come to boarding school.'

She sounded rather forlorn, and some of the others felt sorry for her.

Susan asked kindly, 'Do you live with your aunt?'

'Yes, and my two cousins,' answered Delia, closing her night case firmly. 'My father is a sailor, you see, so he is away a lot, and I have no mother. I don't think that my aunt really wanted me to live with her, and my cousins certainly didn't, for they never made me feel very welcome.'

'What a shame!' said the kind-hearted Pam, touched. 'I daresay you will be glad to be away from them.'

Delia nodded and said, 'Though I can't really blame them for being impatient with me at times. I'm such a duffer!'

The others didn't know quite what to say to this, and were relieved when Bonnie and Amy joined them.

The two newcomers were introduced to the new girls, then Felicity said, 'Well, I suppose we had better take our health certificates to Matron. Got yours, Delia? And you, Millicent? Good, well, off we go then.'

The fifth formers trooped off to Matron's room, where they found her busily ticking things off on a list. She looked up as the girls entered, and her plump face broke into a smile.

'Hallo, fifth formers,' she said. 'My goodness, how strange it feels to be saying that to you! It seems like only yesterday that you came in here as giggling, irresponsible first formers.'

'Yes, but all that is behind us now, Matron,' said June, putting on a very grave expression. 'You see before you a group of very sober, responsible individuals indeed.'

Matron laughed, and said, 'Hmm, as far as *you* are concerned, June, I will believe that when I see it. Now, do you all have your health certificates?'

One by one, the girls handed them over, apart from Delia, who opened her night case and began pulling everything out.

'Delia, what *are* you doing?' asked Susan. 'You've only just put everything back in!'

'I can't find my health certificate,' said Delia. 'I'm quite sure that it is in here somewhere.'

'Well, it had better be, my girl,' said Matron sternly. 'Or it's quarantine for you, and I am sure you don't want that.'

Delia certainly *didn't* want that, and began searching more frantically. At last the health certificate was found, tucked inside one of her slippers, and she handed it over with a sigh of relief.

Matron took it and said, 'Off you go now. You are all in the same dormitory, along with Julie and Lucy, and another new girl called Gillian Weaver.'

'Another new girl!' exclaimed Nora, as they left Matron's room and made their way to the dormitory. 'I wonder what she is like?'

The fifth formers soon found out, for when they reached their dormitory Julie and Lucy were already there, and with them was a slim girl, with narrow green eyes and long, pale auburn curls. She was very attractive indeed, and the others looked at her with interest.

'Hallo, you lot!' cried Julie. 'We've been back for ages, and we've got Jack and Sandy all settled in nicely.'

The others greeted them, then Lucy said, 'This is Gillian Weaver, who is joining our form. And I see we have two more new girls!'

There was a flurry of introductions, then Felicity said happily, 'Well, here we are, all back together again for a new term. I wonder what it will bring?'

The first day

There was just time before tea to show the new girls round a bit. The fifth formers looked in at their new common-room, before going down to the stables, to greet Jack and Sandy.

Delia and Millicent seemed rather nervous of horses and admired them from a distance, but Gillian patted their velvety muzzles and made a great fuss of them.

'Do you ride, Gillian?' asked Julie.

'A little,' said the girl. 'But I don't have much time for it, with my other interests.'

'Oh?' said Lucy. 'And what are they?'

'Well, I simply love tennis,' said Gillian. 'And I see that the courts here are super, so I'm hoping to do well at that this term. And I play the violin, too, and that takes up a lot of my time.'

Millicent's ears pricked up at this, and she said, 'I am a musician myself, and play several instruments, including the violin. Have you taken any music exams?'

'Oh, no,' said Gillian, looking quite alarmed at the thought. 'I simply play for fun.'

Millicent, who took her music very seriously indeed, looked rather disapproving at this, but the others rather liked Gillian, and Freddie took her arm, saying, 'Let's go and take a look at the swimming-pool before tea. There's just time.'

Both Gillian and Millicent went into raptures over the beautiful, natural swimming-pool, which was hollowed out of rocks and filled by the sea.

'Lovely!' exclaimed Gillian. 'I simply can't wait to go for a swim in there.'

'How beautiful,' said Millicent, in her low, dramatic voice. 'It makes me feel like composing a tune, all about the wildness and beauty of the sea.'

'Does it?' said the forthright June, sounding unimpressed. 'It makes me feel like diving in fully clothed, but as I'm a fifth former now, I suppose I shall have to restrain myself.'

Just then the bell went for tea, and Pam cried, 'Good, I'm simply starving. Come along, everyone!'

The fifth formers looked around as they entered the big dining-room, giving rather superior smiles as they saw the lower forms, who all had a mistress seated at the head of their table.

The fifth and sixth formers, however, were judged to be grown-up enough to supervise themselves at meal-times, and ate alone.

'My word, this looks good,' said Susan, rubbing her hands together, as the girls took their seats. 'Cold ham, tomatoes, potatoes cooked in their jackets – and fruit salad with cream for afters. Scrumptious!'

As the fifth formers tucked in, the old girls pointed

out various mistresses to the new girls.

'That's Mam'zelle Rougier over there, at the second formers' table,' said Felicity. 'One of our French mistresses. She can be awfully bad-tempered, so it's best not to get on the wrong side of her.'

'And there is Mam'zelle Dupont, our other French mistress,' said Freddie. 'She's awfully good-hearted, though she has a hot temper at times. And she's a most marvellous person to play tricks on, for she is so easy to take in.'

'Not that *we* shall be playing tricks on her, of course,' said Susan, in a lofty tone. 'We shall leave that sort of thing to the lower school.'

'I can't see Miss James anywhere,' said Nora, peering round. Then she turned to the new girls, and said, 'Miss James is our form mistress. I don't know her awfully well, but she seems quite a good sort.'

'I think that she is coming back later tonight,' said Pam. 'So we will meet her properly for the first time tomorrow.'

'And where is the music master, or mistress?' asked Millicent.

'Well, not all of the girls take music lessons,' explained Felicity. 'So we have someone who comes in several times a week and gives lessons. Her name is Miss Johnston and she's supposed to be awfully good.'

'Yes, I took piano lessons with her for a while back in the second form,' said Pam. 'She's a fine teacher.'

Millicent didn't look impressed by this, and gave a

sniff. 'I daresay I shall be above the standard that she is used to teaching,' she said, rather haughtily. 'But as I have learned just about all there is to learn, perhaps it doesn't matter so very much. As long as I can get my practice in, that is the most important thing.'

The fifth formers exchanged glances, and June said smoothly, 'Perhaps you will be able to teach Miss Johnston a thing or two, Millicent.'

The others grinned, but Millicent, apparently unconscious of any sarcasm, seemed to see this as a compliment, and smiled.

'Will you be taking music lessons, Gillian?' asked Lucy.

Gillian shook her auburn curls, and said, 'No, I stopped taking lessons last year. I have brought my violin to school with me, and I love playing it, but, as I said, it is just for fun.'

Seeing that Delia looked rather left out, Felicity turned to her and said kindly, 'What about you, Delia? Do you have any amazing talents? Are you marvellous at games, or do you play an instrument, or anything?'

'No,' said Delia rather bleakly. 'I'm afraid there's nothing marvellous about me. I'm no good at games, I have no talent for music, and I'm not even very clever at my lessons. I'm just a complete duffer.'

Nora patted the girl on the back, and said, 'Cheer up! I'm jolly pleased to have you here, for it means that you may be bottom of the form once in a while, instead of me.'

The others laughed at this, even Delia herself, and

Susan murmured to Felicity, 'At least she has a sense of humour, and can take a joke. She seems quite nice, although she doesn't have much confidence in herself.'

'And Millicent has too much!' said Felicity. 'I think I like Gillian best, out of the three new girls. She seems natural, and friendly, and good fun.'

The fifth formers were allowed to go to bed when they pleased, within reason, and all of them felt very grown-up and were determined to take advantage of this.

But most of the girls had had very long journeys, and it wasn't long before some of them began to yawn.

'I think that I shall go up soon,' said Nora. 'Otherwise I shall never be able to concentrate in class tomorrow.'

Several of the others felt the same, and got to their feet, and Susan said to Millicent, 'Are you coming to bed?'

Millicent, who was engrossed in a newspaper that she had found on the table, said rather absently, 'I shall stay up a little while longer, I think.'

'What's that you're reading?' asked Pam, curiously. 'It certainly seems to have got your attention.'

Millicent looked up, and said, 'Actually it's an article about a competition to find the best school orchestra in the country. And there is an entry form here too. I was just wondering if I could persuade Miss Grayling to let me get up a Malory Towers orchestra and enter. What do you think?'

The others thought that this sounded like an

extremely exciting idea, and Felicity said, 'I should think that Miss Grayling would be very interested indeed. It's certainly worth asking her, Millicent.'

'Very well,' said Millicent, removing the page she had been reading from the newspaper and folding it carefully. 'I shall ask her tomorrow, then.'

By ten o'clock all of the fifth formers were tucked up in bed, most of them fast asleep.

Only Millicent and Delia seemed to be having trouble in settling down.

Millicent's head was full of dreams of winning the school orchestra competition, of bringing glory to Malory Towers and of having her name spoken with awe by the others.

Delia's feelings were mixed. She felt happy to be away from her mean-spirited aunt and spiteful cousins, but was anxious about whether she would fit in at Malory Towers. She liked the girls, who all seemed very friendly and jolly, and had certainly done their utmost to make her feel welcome. But she was worried that she wouldn't be able to keep up with them at lessons, or games. If only she had a special talent, like Millicent, or Gillian, she might feel like a more worthwhile person. But poor Delia was not gifted at all.

At last, though, she fell asleep, as did Millicent, and soon the only sound coming from the dormitory was Pam's gentle snoring.

After breakfast on the first morning, the new girls had to go and see Miss Grayling, the wise and kindly

Head mistress of Malory Towers. Gillian, Millicent and Delia all felt very nervous as they stood before her, thinking that she looked rather stern. But then Miss Grayling's face broke into a lovely smile, and the three girls relaxed a little as she spoke to them one by one, asking their names.

Then Miss Grayling gave the little speech that she gave to all the new girls at the beginning of term, and the three of them listened intently, feeling very stirred by her words.

At last the Head finished, saying, 'You may go to your classroom now, and please remember what I have said throughout your time at Malory Towers.'

The girls nodded solemnly, and Gillian and Delia turned towards the door. But Millicent lingered, and said rather hesitantly, 'May I ask you something, please, Miss Grayling?'

'Of course,' said the Head. 'What is it, Millicent?'

Millicent told the Head about the school orchestra competition, pleased that she seemed to be listening with as much interest as the girls had listened to her speech earlier.

At last Miss Grayling said, 'I must say that it sounds like a very good idea. We have several very talented musicians at Malory Towers, from various forms, and it would be good for them all to work together at something. Yes, Millicent, you have my permission to get an orchestra together and enter it into the competition. I suggest that you put something up on the notice-boards, then any girl who is interested can put her name down.'

'Thank you, Miss Grayling,' said Millicent, the smile that she gave making her face look much less grave than usual. 'I shall do my very best to make sure that we win.'

'I am sure that you will,' said the Head. 'But even if you don't, I hope that everyone who takes part will learn something of value from the experience.'

Millicent was rather puzzled by this. What on earth was the point of entering a competition just to learn something from it? She was going to go all out to make sure that the Malory Towers orchestra – *her* Malory Towers orchestra – won, for that was the whole point. Of course, she didn't say this to Miss Grayling, but went along to the classroom with her head full of plans.

The other girls were already seated, and Millicent took the only seat that was left, in the front row, with Gillian and Delia.

Miss James had not yet arrived, and June said, 'Did you ask the Head about the competition, Millicent?'

'Yes, and she's given permission,' said Millicent, looking and sounding more excited than the girls had yet seen her. 'Gillian, you must let me hear you play your violin, for there may be a place for you in the orchestra. And Pam, didn't you say that you could play the piano?'

'Yes,' answered Pam, looking rather doubtful. 'But I don't know that I'm good enough to play in an orchestra.'

'Well, we'll soon see,' said Millicent. 'I am going to put something up on the notice-board a little later, and I will be holding auditions for anyone who is interested.'

'To be honest, I don't know whether I *want* to be in the orchestra,' murmured Pam to Nora. 'I rather fancied a nice, easy term.'

'Well, just fluff your audition,' said Nora. 'Then Millicent won't want you.'

Just then Miss James's footsteps could be heard approaching, and the girls fell silent, while Susan got up to hold the door open for the mistress.

'Thank you, Susan,' said Miss James, with a smile. 'Please sit down, girls.'

The girls sat, and looked at Miss James curiously. She was tall and thin, with curly grey hair and hazel eyes. Delia thought that she looked kind, and felt much more comfortable.

'Well, before we get down to the business of making out time-tables, there are one or two matters I need to tell you about,' said the mistress. 'First of all, I am sure that you are all eager to know who is to be head of the form. This is something that I discussed with Miss Potts and Miss Williams, who was your form mistress last year, and I took their advice before making my decision.'

Miss James had, in fact, had a very long discussion with the two mistresses.

'Susan Blake was head of the form last term,' Miss

Williams had said. 'And very good she was too. I believe that Felicity Rivers was an excellent head-girl in the third form as well.'

'Either of them would be a good choice,' Miss Potts, the head of North Tower, had said. 'But I have a very strong feeling that Miss Grayling may make one of them Head Girl when they go up into the sixth next year. As you know, the Head Girl of the sixth will be Head Girl of the whole school. So it seems to me that someone else should have the honour this year.'

Miss James had nodded, and ran her eye over the list of names in front of her.

'Nora Woods,' she had said aloud.

'No!' Miss Potts and Miss Williams had said at once.

'Nora is a dear girl,' said Miss Williams. 'But a complete scatter-brain.'

'I think that you can also rule out Amy and Bonnie,' said Miss Potts. 'Neither of them has the makings of a leader.'

'June?' suggested Miss Williams.

'Ah, now June most definitely *is* a leader,' said Miss Potts. 'Though she is not always very kind at times. Besides, Miss Grayling and I have other plans for June.'

Miss Williams and Miss James exchanged curious glances, but Miss Potts would not be drawn, and went on to say, 'Freddie will always follow June's lead, so I don't think that she would be a good head-girl either. That leaves Pam, Julie and Lucy.'

'All nice girls, with good characters,' said Miss

Williams. 'But Julie and Lucy are so horse-mad that there is very little time for anything else in their lives, and I don't think that either of them would be very whole-hearted about being head of the form.'

'Pam was head-girl in the second form,' said Miss Potts. 'All of the girls like, trust and respect her.'

'Well, it looks like Pam will be head of the fifth form, then,' said Miss James.

Now Miss James made the announcement in class, and all of the fifth formers were delighted. Had they been in a lower form, there would have been an outbreak of cheering and clapping, but as fifth formers they were more restrained, saying, 'Well done, Pam, old girl.'

'Yes, jolly good choice.'

'You'll make a fine head-girl.'

'Oh gosh!' said Pam, feeling quite overwhelmed. 'Just as I was saying that I fancied an easy term.'

But, of course, she was as pleased as punch, and simply couldn't wait to write to her parents and tell them the good news.

Miss James smiled, and said, 'I have something else to tell you, as well. As you know, Ruth Grainger, the games captain, left Malory Towers last term. As there is no one in the sixth form who is really good enough to take her place, the new captain is going to be someone from the fifth form – June!'

For a moment June thought that she hadn't heard properly, for surely Miss James couldn't have said that she was to be games captain of the whole *school*? But the others were beaming at her, congratulating her, and Freddie was clapping her on the back, so it *must* be true!

June was both astonished and delighted, for it had never occurred to her that she would ever be given a position of responsibility at Malory Towers. It was true that she was far and away the best sportswoman in the school. But she also had a reputation for being bold, mischievous and downright wicked at times!

Miss Potts had said as much to Miss Grayling when they had talked about the matter, and Miss Grayling had said, 'Well, it is time for June to put her tricks and jokes behind her, and learn how to be a responsible young woman. There is no doubt at all that she has the drive and determination to succeed, and I feel that this could be the making of her.'

And it seemed that June was going to make the most of the opportunity offered to her, for she was already turning over various plans in her mind.

The Malory Towers teams were going to win every tennis match they went in for. She would arrange extra coaching for the lower forms, and pick out any promising youngsters. And woe betide any slackers! Even people like Bonnie and Amy, who simply loathed games, would have to toe the line.

But there was no time to think about that now, for Miss James was speaking again, saying, 'Of course, it is a very big responsibility for one person alone, so Felicity and Susan will help you.'

Felicity and Susan exchanged excited glances, both of

them wishing for a moment that they were back in the first form so that they could let out a yell! Goodness, what a term this was going to be!

A clash of wills

'Well, what a morning it's been!' exclaimed Felicity, as the fifth formers went out into the fresh air at break-time. 'Pam head of the form, June head of games for the whole school, and Millicent has been given permission to get up an orchestra.'

'Where *is* Millicent?' asked Susan, looking round.

'Oh, she's gone off to write out a notice, so that people will get to know about the auditions she is holding,' said Nora. 'I must say she's awfully keen. How about you, June? I'm surprised that you haven't started making out lists of teams yet, or putting up notices about practice times.'

June laughed, and said, 'Well, I have a lot more to think about than Millicent. All she has to do is listen to people play, and decide whether they are good enough or not. After that, it is simply a matter of rehearsing. I have to arrange matches and practices, decide on players and reserves, coach people, and do my best to bring all the slackers up to scratch!'

'Well, thank goodness you have two willing helpers,' said Julie.

'Yes, I think the three of us will work together well,'

said June, grinning at Felicity and Susan. 'Perhaps we can put our heads together in the common-room later, and decide how we are going to go about this?'

Felicity and Susan nodded eagerly, then June turned to Gillian and said, 'If you are as good at tennis as you say, you might get a place on one of the teams. It's tennis next lesson, so I shall be watching you carefully.'

Not only did June get the opportunity to watch Gillian, she actually played against her. And she soon saw that the new girl was as good as her word, for Gillian was a marvellous player and very nearly beat June. And, for once, June didn't mind, for she was absolutely thrilled to have found someone who could play tennis so well.

'You're a certainty for the team!' said June, in the changing-room afterwards. 'Just make sure that you keep your practice up.'

'Heavens, I am in demand!' said Gillian, with a laugh. 'Millicent wants me to try out for her orchestra, and now you want me to play tennis.'

'What it is to be popular!' laughed Freddie. 'What are you going to do, Gillian?'

'Well, it's quite obvious that Gillian will choose to play tennis,' said June. 'Who wants to play in a stuffy orchestra, when they can be out in the fresh air.'

Unfortunately, Millicent overheard this, and said stiffly, 'There will be nothing stuffy about the Malory Towers orchestra, June. I simply can't imagine why Gillian would want to waste her time knocking a ball back and forth, when she could be using her talent for something worthwhile.'

June opened her mouth to retort, but Bonnie interrupted to say, 'Millicent, you haven't even heard Gillian play yet. You only have her word for it that she is any good.'

This was very true, and Millicent said, 'Well, there is a little spare time before lunch. Why don't you go and fetch your violin, Gillian, and you can play for us in the common-room now?'

So Gillian sped off to get her violin from the dormitory, while the others gathered expectantly in the common-room. When the new girl came back, she had loosened her long curls from the ribbon that had been tying them back, and when Freddie asked why, Gillian said, 'I always wear my hair loose when I play the violin. It makes me feel more artistic somehow.'

Then the girl placed the violin under her chin and began to play. And what a performance she gave! The fifth formers listened, enthralled, as Gillian played, her bow darting over the strings, her enjoyment clear, as beautiful music filled the room. It was quite clear that Gillian had not exaggerated at all, and was a first-class violinist. When she finished, the girls clapped and cheered like mad.

'Simply beautiful!'

'Top-hole! Gillian, you're a marvel.'

'Millicent, you simply must put her in the orchestra.'

'I shall,' said Millicent, pleased to have found someone so talented.

Only June said nothing. She, too, had been impressed by Gillian's playing, but she badly wanted the girl to be on one of the tennis teams, and she had no intention of allowing Millicent to steal her away.

'Well, Gillian, it looks as if you must make a choice,' said Pam.

'Yes, I suppose I must,' said Gillian, with a grimace. 'If you don't mind, June and Millicent, I should like to think about it for a while.'

'Well, don't think about it for too long,' said Millicent, rather coolly. 'I need to choose my orchestra, and lick it into shape. There is no time to waste.'

June, watching Millicent closely, decided that the girl was going to be a bit of a slave-driver, and could see that she ran the risk of making herself very unpopular with her orchestra if she pushed them too hard. She herself said pleasantly, 'Of course, Gillian, you take your time. There's no hurry for you to make up your mind, and I want you to be sure that you have made the right choice.'

The rest of the fifth form stared at June hard. They knew her very well indeed, and if June wanted something badly, she didn't give up without a fight.

When the fifth formers went into the dining-room for lunch, it seemed that word had got around that June was the new games captain, for many of the younger girls nudged one another and whispered as she walked by.

Hannah, of the second form, came up to her, and said shyly, 'Congratulations, June. We second formers are simply thrilled that you are our new games captain.'

'Thanks, kid,' said June, in her usual careless way, though she was secretly delighted and rather touched by this. 'You're Hannah, aren't you? I remember watching you play last year, when you were in the first form. I hope that you are going to try out for one of the teams this term, for you were pretty good.'

Hannah, so overwhelmed that she was quite unable to speak, merely nodded, before rushing back to her table to tell the second formers that the great June had asked her to try out for one of the teams.

Millicent, meanwhile, had watched the little by-play with a sour expression, and wondered if she would be able to inspire the same devotion in her orchestra.

She had certainly stirred people's interest, for many girls, from different forms and different towers, put their names on the list that she had pinned up, and Millicent decided to hold auditions on the first Saturday of the term.

Auditions were being held in the big hall, and the rest of the fifth formers went along to watch.

'There's nothing better to do,' said June, looking at the gloomy weather outside the window, and sighing. 'I had planned to hold tennis practice for the lower forms, but it's going to pour down any minute.'

The fifth formers had to sit right at the back of the hall, for it seemed that half of the school had decided that watching the auditions would be a pleasant way to while away a rainy afternoon.

Millicent stepped on to the stage, a list of names in

her hand, and she called out, 'Pam, would you like to sit at the piano and go first?'

Pulling a face at Nora, Pam walked to the front of the hall, where the piano stood, and sat down at it. She played a simple piece of music that she knew well, and, although she had intended to play a few wrong notes and spoil her chances of getting into the orchestra, found that she couldn't, as the music took hold of her. It was a pleasant performance, and the listening girls clapped, but Millicent merely said, 'Not bad. Hannah Dixon, you play the piano, don't you? Let's see if you can do any better.'

June, sitting next to Freddie, gasped as Hannah of the second form got up, and whispered, 'Millicent is doing this on purpose! She heard me telling Hannah that I wanted her to practise hard at her tennis, and this is her way of getting back at me. I bet you anything you like that she picks Hannah to be in her precious orchestra!'

'Yes, but you can't blame Millicent entirely,' Freddie whispered back. 'Hannah must have put her name on the list in the first place.'

'Not necessarily,' said June. 'Pam didn't put her name down, but Millicent badgered her into playing anyway.'

'Can whoever is whispering please be quiet?' said Millicent sharply. 'It really is very rude when Hannah is waiting to begin.'

Millicent knew very well that it was June who was whispering, but there was an unwritten rule among the fifth formers that they did not find fault with one another in front of the younger girls.

But although Millicent hadn't named her, June was annoyed. Really, Millicent would do well to remember that she was a new girl!

Hannah played very well indeed, and Millicent gave her a word of praise when she finished her piece.

'Very good,' she said. 'I shall certainly consider you as our pianist, Hannah, though I can't say anything definite until I have heard the others.'

Several more musicians took to the stage, playing a variety of instruments. One girl played the flute, another the trumpet, and yet another the cello. There were several more pianists, too, as well as four or five violinists. Then Gillian got up, holding her violin, and Millicent said, 'There is no need for you to audition, Gillian, for I heard you play the other day.'

'I know, but I am in a musical mood today, and felt like playing my violin anyway, so I thought that I would play the tune that I played in the common-room the other day.'

To everyone's surprise, Millicent smiled and said, 'Well, that will certainly be a treat for everyone. I know that tune, so if you don't mind, I will accompany you on the piano.'

'For all her boasting about what a wonderful musician she is, I've never heard Millicent play anything,' murmured Pam to Nora. 'Now we shall see how good she really is.'

As it turned out, Millicent was very good indeed. She and Gillian held the watching girls spellbound, and several of the younger girls found tears starting to their eyes, the music was so lovely. When they finished, everyone got to their feet and clapped so hard that Felicity thought they would raise the roof!

Even June had to admit grudgingly, 'She certainly plays the piano brilliantly. In fact, she is so brilliant that I wonder she doesn't give herself the job as pianist in her orchestra. Then she can leave Hannah out of it.'

The same thought occurred to Pam, but when she suggested it to Millicent after the auditions were over, the girl said, 'I can't, for I shall be conducting, you see. I learned how to do that at the music academy, and while we have several good pianists, I doubt if there is anyone here who knows how to conduct.'

This was very true, so it seemed that one of the girls who had auditioned would have to become the orchestra pianist. Pam felt quite confident that she would not be chosen, for she had been outshone by several other girls, including young Hannah.

Seeing Millicent hunched up over a table in the common-room that evening, busily writing some kind of list, Felicity called out, 'Have you decided who is to be in the orchestra yet, Millicent?'

'I have decided on several people, but there are one or two that I haven't quite made up my mind about,' said the girl. 'I am going to decide by tomorrow, then we shall be able to call the first rehearsal. Gillian, you are in – if you want to be. But you really must let me know by tomorrow.'

'Have you decided what piece you are going to play?' asked Susan, looking up from the book she was reading.

'Yes, I am going to teach the girls a composition of my own,' answered Millicent, sounding rather smug. 'I wrote it last term at the music academy, and my teachers there thought that it was quite outstanding.'

Then Millicent spotted June looking at her with dislike, and said, 'What bad luck that you couldn't hold your tennis practice earlier, June. That's the beauty of music, you see. No matter what the weather, one can still play.'

June bit back a sharp retort, made her expression perfectly bland, and said airily, 'It doesn't matter. The weather will improve soon, and then my tennis practices will go ahead. The youngsters do so enjoy spending as much time as possible in the fresh air during the summer months.'

As it happened, the weather cleared the very next day, and the girls awoke to bright sunshine. Immediately after breakfast, June put a notice on the board to say that she would be holding tennis practice for the lower school at two o'clock. And, when the time came, she, Felicity and Susan were delighted to see that there was a good turn out.

The lower school had always looked up to June, admiring her boldness, her outspoken manner, and her reputation for playing tricks. Now that she was their games captain, many of them almost worshipped her.

Hannah was there, and June greeted her with a smile,

saying, 'I'm glad to see you here, Hannah. When I saw you playing the piano for Millicent yesterday, I was afraid that you might have decided to join the orchestra instead of playing tennis for the school.'

'Well, I put my name on Millicent's list as soon as she pinned it up, and that was before you told me that I might have a chance of getting on to the team, June.' Hannah looked up at the bigger girl and said, 'Of course, I would much rather play tennis, if you think that I am good enough, and if Millicent does want me for her orchestra I am going to say no.'

June was delighted to hear this, and she gave Hannah a clap on the shoulder.

As the second former walked away to take her place on the court, Felicity came up to June, and said, 'You look pleased with yourself.'

'I am,' said June. 'Hannah has told me that she would rather play tennis than be in Millicent's orchestra.'

'I see,' said Felicity. 'And are you pleased because you have a good player for the lower-school team, or because you have got one over on Millicent?'

June laughed, and said, 'Both. Don't worry, Felicity, I know what you're thinking, and I don't intend to let my dislike of Millicent interfere with any decisions I make as games captain. Believe it or not, I am taking my responsibilities very seriously.'

Felicity was pleased to hear this, and she and Susan felt heartened to see June taking so much trouble over the youngsters. June gave a word of praise here, and criticised there. But, Felicity noticed, whenever June made a criticism, she always told the girl she was talking to how to put matters right.

'Who would have thought it!' said Susan, as she watched June showing a little first former how to serve. 'Perhaps June is mellowing in her old age.'

'I think the fact that these kids look up to her no end helps,' said Felicity. 'They really do adore her, and June is basking in it. I just hope that she doesn't get a swollen head!'

'I don't think that she will,' said Susan. 'June is too downright to let all this hero-worship go to her head. My word, some of these kids are jolly good! Look at little Maggie there. She might be tiny, but she's jolly fierce.'

June came over to them then, a smile on her face as she said, 'Some promising players out there, don't you think?'

'That's exactly what I was just saying,' said Susan. 'We certainly have plenty of talent to choose from when it comes to the lower-school team.'

'We should do well with the upper-school team as well,' said June. 'You two will be playing, of course.'

Both girls gasped and looked at one another with shining eyes, then Felicity said, 'June, you don't have to put us in the team simply because we are helping you with your games captain's duties, you know.'

'I'm not,' said June. 'I'm choosing you because you happen to be two of the best players in the school.'

'Thanks!' said Susan, quite taken aback at this unexpected praise from June.

'I desperately want Gillian, too,' said June, her eyes narrowing. 'I shall be so disappointed if she takes up Millicent's offer of a place in the orchestra instead. I wonder if she has made her mind up yet?'

Gillian had, and she announced her decision in the common-room that very evening.

'June,' she said. 'I have decided that I would like to take up your offer of a place on the upper-school team.'

June's face lit up and she was quite unable to help shooting a look of triumph at Millicent, who looked as glum as could be.

But Gillian hadn't finished, for she went on, 'And Millicent, I should also like to play the violin in your orchestra, if I may.'

Everyone looked most surprised, and it was left to Pam, as head of the form, to say, 'But Gillian, you can't possibly do both! Why, you'll wear yourself out completely and you won't be able to concentrate on your lessons.'

'But I am being offered the chance to have fun doing the two things that I love most, so how can I possibly choose one over the other?' said Gillian. 'Don't worry about me, Pam, for I shall be perfectly fine.'

'I hope so,' said Pam, sounding extremely doubtful. 'But if it becomes too much for you, Gillian, you will simply have to give one up.'

June glanced across at Millicent, and their eyes met in a hostile look. June was thinking that if Gillian was going to give anything up it would be the violin. And Millicent was thinking that if Gillian had to eventually make a choice, she was determined that the girl was going to choose her orchestra!

An interesting rehearsal

What with one thing and another, life was very busy at Malory Towers. Millicent had chosen the girls who were to be in her orchestra, and had given them all copies of the piece of music she had written.

She had asked Hannah to be the pianist, but, feeling a little nervous, Hannah had said haltingly, 'I feel very honoured that you have asked me, Millicent, but I have decided to work hard at my tennis for June, instead.'

Millicent had looked at Hannah so coldly that the second former's knees shook, and she feared that she was about to get a scold. But Millicent merely said, 'Very well, Hannah, if that is your decision. I hope that you have made the right choice.'

Then she had gone off to find Anne, a fifth former from South Tower, and asked her if she would like to play the piano instead. Anne had been absolutely thrilled, and so grateful for the opportunity that Millicent cheered up a bit. And she was further gratified when she walked by the little music rooms that the girls used for practising in, and heard her own composition being played. All of the musicians were working very hard indeed, and Millicent really didn't see how Malory

Towers could fail to win the competition.

Delia came along the corridor as Millicent stood outside one of the music-rooms, listening to Anne rehearsing her piano solo, and she said, 'Is that the music that you wrote, Millicent? My word, you really do have a gift. How I envy you. All everyone seems to talk about at the moment is tennis, or the orchestra, but I can't contribute anything because I'm hopeless at games and no good at music. Why, when I sing at home, my aunt says it sounds like a cat yowling.'

Millicent wasn't much given to considering anyone else's feelings, but there was something so wistful in Delia's tone that she felt rather touched, and said kindly, 'Well, there are other ways you could be involved, you know, Delia. I could certainly do with someone to assist me at rehearsals, to make notes and so on.'

'Really?' said Delia, her face lighting up. 'Would you trust me to do that, Millicent?'

'Of course,' said Millicent. 'Now listen, Delia, the first rehearsal is on Tuesday, after tea, in the hall. So just you come along and I'm sure that I will find plenty for you to do.'

Delia nodded eagerly, and both girls went their separate ways, Delia thrilled to think that she was going to play a part in the orchestra's success, and Millicent feeling that she had done something very good and virtuous.

June, somewhat to her own surprise, was thoroughly enjoying coaching the youngsters at tennis. The upper school were more of a challenge, however, and in the end she abandoned her plans to make people like Amy and Bonnie attend regular practices.

'I really don't know why you bother,' said Felicity, one day, after watching a long and fruitless argument between June and Bonnie, which had ended with the latter flatly refusing to come to practice. 'You are never going to make a tennis player out of Bonnie, or Amy, for that matter, so you may as well give up.'

But June was extremely stubborn when she had set her mind to something, and continued to badger Amy and Bonnie.

'She's so persistent!' Amy complained. 'Honestly, Bonnie, sometimes I feel like giving up and going to her wretched tennis practice just so that she will leave me alone.'

But Bonnie could be stubborn too, and she shook her head, saying, 'We mustn't give in to June, or she will become even worse. I shall come up with a plan to make her leave us alone.'

In fact it was June herself who gave Bonnie an idea. She had been inspecting the white tennis dresses that the Malory Towers girls wore when they played matches against other schools, and discovered that some of them were very shabby indeed.

'Hems coming down, pockets ripped and holes in seams,' she complained in the common-room one evening. 'I can't send our teams off to play in those! We'll be a laughing stock!'

Bonnie, who had been listening intently, approached

June later, and said, 'I want to make a bargain with you. I will repair all of the tennis dresses and make them as good as new.'

June's eyes lit up, and she said, 'Would you really do that? Bonnie, you're an angel.'

'Yes, but I want something in return,' said Bonnie, before June got too carried away. 'You are to leave Amy and me alone, and not try to get us to play tennis.'

June looked down into Bonnie's sweet little face, and gave a reluctant laugh. 'You can be every bit as determined as me when you want something, can't you?' she said. 'Or when you want to get *out* of something! Well, it really would be a help to me if you would mend the dresses, Bonnie. I suppose, in your way, you will be doing your bit for the team.'

So the bargain was struck, and Bonnie, sticking to her side of it, began work on the dresses at once. Not only did she repair hems and mend seams, with her neat, tiny stitches, but she painstakingly embroidered the initials M and T, for Malory Towers, on the pocket of each dress, in deep orange.

June was thrilled, and cried, 'Bonnie, you're marvellous! Our players will look as neat as new pins now, and I shall be proud to watch them play.'

Bonnie accepted the praise graciously, but really she had thoroughly enjoyed working on the dresses, for needlework was her favourite pastime.

Millicent, who had felt extremely jealous of the smart tennis dresses that June's teams would be wearing, overheard this. All of the orchestras in the competition would be wearing their school uniforms, but Millicent had been trying to think of something that would make the Malory Towers girls stand out. Now she had a sudden brainwave, and she turned to Bonnie, saying, 'I have a project for you, Bonnie, if you're willing.'

'What is it?' asked Bonnie curiously.

'Well,' said Millicent. 'It occurred to me that it would be nice if each member of our orchestra had a pennant to hang from her music stand. Perhaps –'

'Yes,' interrupted Bonnie excitedly, her creative mind grasping the idea at once. 'I see exactly how they should look! Triangular pennants made from orange fabric, with the letters M and T embroidered in brown, so that the colours match the school uniform. How does that sound, Millicent?'

'That sounds super!' said Millicent, who hadn't got as far as thinking about the colours. 'Bonnie, would you be able to do that? If you can, I shall owe you a favour.'

Of course, Bonnie was only too pleased to help out, for she was thrilled to have a new project to work on, and she always liked being in a position where someone owed her a favour.

So Bonnie felt as if she was really doing rather a lot to help both June and Millicent. Alas for poor Delia, however; her efforts to assist Millicent did not get off to a good start.

The orchestra held their first proper rehearsal together in the big hall, and Delia made sure that all the music stands had a copy of Millicent's score there, ready and waiting.

'Thank you, Delia,' said Millicent, as she led the orchestra into the hall. 'Now, what I would like you to do is sit at the side there, and jot down any comments and suggestions I make in a notebook. Later I shall be able to read them back and make any improvements that are needed to the score. See?'

Delia nodded eagerly, and took her seat, notebook and pen at the ready.

Millicent stood in front of the orchestra, baton in hand and conducted. But, when the music stopped, she had a great many criticisms to make, for this was the first time that the orchestra had played together, and, naturally, mistakes were made. Delia was most assiduous in recording all of Millicent's remarks.

'Anne!' said Millicent sharply. 'You played two wrong notes in your solo. You really must try to do better! And Janet, you came in far too late. A mistake like that could cost us the competition. As for the violins, it was simply dreadful! Gillian was the only one of you who played perfectly. I suggest that you all spend some time rehearsing together.'

The girls knew only too well that they had made mistakes, but they rather resented Millicent's high-handed attitude.

'I don't mind having my mistakes pointed out,' muttered Janet. 'But she could be a little more polite and pleasant about it.'

Helen, one of the violinists, nodded in agreement and whispered, 'I do think she's awfully hard on us. After all, it is the first time that we have all played together. She can't expect us to be perfect!'

But it seemed that this was exactly what Millicent did expect. She made Anne play her piano solo again, and when the girl played the same two wrong notes, Millicent scolded her so harshly that she was almost reduced to tears.

'What a pity that Hannah didn't want to be pianist,' Millicent remarked scathingly. 'At least she would have taken the trouble to learn the music before turning up for rehearsal.'

Anne, who hadn't realised that Hannah had been first choice, felt very upset indeed.

For a moment she considered walking off, but she so badly wanted to be a part of the orchestra, and had already written to her parents about it. So poor Anne swallowed her pride, and stayed where she was.

But many of the others sent silent glances of sympathy Anne's way, and glared at Millicent. Unfortunately for them, Millicent, who could be very thick-skinned at times, didn't even notice.

When the orchestra played the piece for the second time, it sounded much better, to Delia's untrained ear. Quite beautiful, in fact. Millicent did not agree, and continued to criticise and suggest improvements, but Delia, who had become quite lost in the music, completely forgot to write them down. The piece that

Millicent had composed was called 'Summer Serenade' and, as she listened, Delia thought that it really did capture the essence of summer perfectly, making her think of picnics, and walks along the beach.

Quite suddenly, words began to form in her head, that fitted in with the music, and, turning hastily to the back of the notebook Delia began to jot them down. Millicent, glancing across, saw the girl scribbling away, and felt satisfied that the was doing her job properly.

But Delia's sudden burst of creativity ended, and she closed the notebook as Millicent lowered her baton and spoke to the orchestra.

'Better, but not good enough!' she said, a stern expression on her face. 'I expect you all to practise until you are perfect before the next rehearsal.'

The only person who came in for unstinted praise was Gillian, and Janet remarked rather bitterly, 'Of course, the two of them are in the same form and the same tower, so Millicent is bound to favour her. I expect that the two of them are friends.'

In fact, Gillian had decided that she didn't like Millicent much at all. She thought the girl high-handed and rather humourless, and hadn't cared for some of the unkind remarks that she had made to the others.

She really doesn't know how to get the best out of people, thought Gillian, as she put her violin away. All that Millicent has done is make everyone feel terribly nervous, for now we all know that we are in for a tongue lashing if we make a mistake.

Delia, who had remained behind to collect the scores that had been left on the music stands, went across to Gillian and said a little shyly, 'You played awfully well, Gillian.'

Gillian smiled. She liked the rather sweet-natured, awkward Delia. 'Thank you,' she said. 'Though I can't help wishing that Millicent had praised some of the others as much as she praised me. I have a feeling that her sharp tongue is going to cause problems.'

'I think that she just wants everything to be perfect,' said Delia. 'She has her heart set on winning this competition, you know, and I suppose that she feels a lot rests on her shoulders, as she wrote the music as well.'

'I daresay you're right,' said Gillian. 'But I do wish that she wasn't quite so intense and serious.'

Delia was quite right about Millicent. She wanted desperately to lead Malory Towers to victory in the orchestra competition, and if they could win playing her very own composition, it would be a huge feather in her cap.

But some of the players simply weren't up to scratch, and it was up to her, Millicent, to see that they improved. She went up to Delia in the common-room that evening, and said, 'I say, Delia, do you have that notebook? I intend to go through it this evening, so that I can see where all the weak spots are.'

Delia handed over the notebook, but Millicent wasn't able to read it that evening, after all, for Matron put her head round the door and cried, 'Millicent Moon! I have a pile of your mending here, which needs to be unpicked and done again.'

Millicent, who didn't like mending at all, turned red and said, 'Sorry, Matron. I'm not very good at sewing, and I'm afraid I rushed it, rather.'

'Well, you will do it again this evening,' said Matron, sternly. 'And this time, Millicent, please do it carefully, for I shall inspect it tomorrow.'

With that, Matron handed Millicent the pile of mending, and shut the door behind her.

Millicent scowled. Blow Matron! She had so wanted to go through that notebook tonight. She wondered if Bonnie could be persuaded to do the mending for her, and glanced across at the girl. But Bonnie was busily engaged in embroidering one of the pennants for the orchestra, and Millicent decided that was far more important than her mending.

'How I hate sewing!' she said aloud, hoping that one of the girls would take pity on her and offer to do it for her. But no one did, for they had all noticed that Millicent often used the excuse of being a musical genius to get out of doing other, more mundane tasks.

Delia wondered if she should offer, though sewing wasn't one of her talents, and she opened her mouth to speak. But Pam caught her eye and gave a small shake of the head, and Delia subsided.

'Well, Millicent,' said Felicity, who was doing a jigsaw with Susan. 'It rather looks as if you are going to have to do your own mending, doesn't it?'

'We never had to do our own mending at the music academy,' said Millicent crossly, getting out her work-basket. 'It is such a waste of time, when I could be working on my piece for the competition.'

'You're getting far too wrapped up in this competition, if you ask me,' said Pam. 'And the mistresses are starting to notice it too. I overheard Miss James telling Miss Potts that she is not very pleased with you, for you don't pay attention in class.'

'Be careful, Millicent,' warned June. 'If Miss Grayling thinks that your involvement with the orchestra is affecting your class-work, she may change her mind and make you pull out.'

Millicent was quite horrified at that thought. She would have to be very careful indeed, and at least try to *look* as if she was paying attention in class.

Yet the very next second, she decided that she would take the notebook into French with her tomorrow, and slip it inside the pages of the book that the form was reading with Mam'zelle Dupont. Mam'zelle was so easy to fool that she would never spot a thing!

Millicent in trouble

Mam'zelle Dupont was in a good mood when she walked into the fifth-form classroom the following morning. She had had a good night's sleep and felt well rested, the sun was shining, and she liked these fifth formers. They were good, hard-working girls, even June, who had been such a bad girl when she was lower down the school.

Nora, one of Mam'zelle's favourites, was holding the door open for her, and the French mistress smiled, and said, '*Merci*, Nora. *Asseyez-vous, s'il vous plait.*'

The fifth formers took their seats, and Mam'zelle beamed round, saying, 'Please open your books, and we will continue reading this so-excellent story. *Ma chère* Felicity, you will begin please.'

As Felicity began reading, Millicent opened her book, into which she had already slipped the notebook. The girl was soon lost in her world of music as she began to read the notes that Delia had written, in her large, untidy handwriting, and she was able to shut out everything around her.

Gillian, who sat beside Millicent, saw what the girl was doing, and thought her very silly indeed. Millicent was going to get into serious trouble if she wasn't careful. But

Gillian couldn't very well say anything to her without attracting unwelcome attention from Mam'zelle.

So Millicent remained engrossed in her music, while the rest of the class read the French book, and no one but Gillian noticed a thing. Until Mam'zelle said, 'Millicent, you will read now, please.'

Of course, Millicent didn't even hear Mam'zelle, not even when the French mistress repeated her instruction. The rest of the fifth formers looked at one another, puzzled, and Gillian gave Millicent a nudge. Then, to her amazement, and the amazement of everyone else in the room, Millicent suddenly let out a roar.

Gillian was extremely startled, for she had barely touched the girl. But it seemed that Millicent's anger was not directed at her, for the girl stood up and yelled, 'Delia, you idiot! What on earth has happened to the notes that you were supposed to be making? You have only written down the remarks that I made after the first run-through, then there is nothing!'

The fifth formers stared at Millicent in astonishment, while poor Delia looked most taken aback. But the most surprised person in the class was Mam'zelle herself, who simply couldn't believe her ears.

Mam'zelle did not care for Millicent, for the girl paid scant attention in class, and acted as if French did not matter – as if nothing mattered, in fact, except her music. And now she dared to disrupt the class with this outburst of temper. Mam'zelle's good mood suddenly vanished, and she cried angrily, 'How dare you behave like this in my class, Millicent!'

Millicent continued to ignore Mam'zelle, who was growing redder and angrier by the second, and carried on with her tirade at Delia, whose knees were now shaking.

The fifth formers had no idea what was the matter with Millicent, whom they thought had gone quite mad, but as the girl was taking no notice at all of Mam'zelle, Pam took a hand in the affair.

She walked across to Millicent and took the girl firmly by the arm, saying sharply, 'Millicent, control yourself at once! You are behaving like a first former, and if you are not careful Mam'zelle will send you to Miss Grayling. Do behave, for heaven's sake.'

The threat of being sent to the Head seemed to snap Millicent out of her rage, for she blinked suddenly and fell silent.

Mam'zelle, taking advantage of the sudden silence, stepped towards her and said, 'Vous êtes insupportable, Millicent! Méchante fille! You will be punished for this extraordinary behaviour.'

'I beg your pardon, Mam'zelle,' gasped Millicent, afraid now, and deciding that the wisest course of action was to apologise profusely to the angry French mistress. 'I simply don't know what came over me.'

Mam'zelle was moving closer, and, in horror, Millicent glanced down at the French book on her desk. If the French mistress spotted the notebook there, she would certainly be sent to the Head, and all her dreams of winning the competition would be shattered. But the notebook was gone! For quick-thinking Gillian, seeing disaster looming for Millicent, had quickly snatched the notebook away as Mam'zelle approached, and hidden it in her satchel. She had no way of informing Millicent of this, though, for Mam'zelle was scolding the girl roundly, in a mixture of French and English, and all that Millicent could do was hang her head and hope that her punishment would not be too severe.

The others watched in fascination, torn between guilty enjoyment at seeing Millicent get into a row, and embarrassment that a fifth former should have behaved in such a way. Had they been in the first or second form, this would have been a very exciting interlude in their day, but as fifth formers they felt slightly ashamed of Millicent. Only June, who saw Millicent as a rival, watched with unalloyed glee, though she would not have admitted this to the others, and made her expression perfectly grave.

At last Mam'zelle seemed to run out of steam, and came to a halt, her chest heaving as she glared angrily at Millicent.

Once again Gillian nudged her, hissing, 'Apologise again, ass! It's your only chance of staying out of trouble.'

Millicent did so, in a very meek manner, stammering slightly and with downcast eyes, and when she peeped at Mam'zelle through her eyelashes, she was relieved to see that the French mistress looked a little calmer.

But Mam'zelle still felt angry with Millicent for her extraordinary outburst, and could not let it pass.

'You will stay behind at break-time, and I shall give you a punishment,' said Mam'zelle sternly. 'And think yourself lucky, Millicent, that I do not send you to Miss Grayling!'

Millicent *did* consider herself lucky, and heaved a sigh of relief. Mam'zelle would be sure to dish out some perfectly horrid punishment, but if she had sent Millicent to the Head it might have ended with her having to pull out of the competition.

At break-time, everyone but Millicent went out into the fresh air, and the fifth formers clustered round Delia.

'What on earth was that all about?' asked Felicity, curiously. 'Millicent seemed angry with *you*, Delia, but I can't think why!'

'I was supposed to note down all her remarks during the last rehearsal,' explained Delia, rather dolefully. 'But halfway through I sort of lost myself in the music and completely forgot to write anything down.'

Delia didn't say that she had been busily jotting down her own words to set to the music, for she felt certain that the others would laugh at her. She felt hot as it suddenly occurred to her that Millicent might find the silly little rhyme written in the back of the notebook, and she made up her mind that she must get hold of it and tear the page out. Millicent had a sharp tongue, and would probably make fun of her. Of course, Delia didn't know that the notebook was now in Gillian's possession.

'Well, anyone can make a mistake,' said Susan, giving Delia a pat on the shoulder. 'Cheer up! Millicent is the one at fault, for she should not have shouted at you like that in front of everyone.'

'And she shouldn't have been reading that notebook in the French lesson,' said Pam, disapprovingly. 'I shall be having words with dear Millicent later.'

Millicent found that the fifth formers were rather cool towards her for the rest of the day, but simply couldn't understand why. The orchestra and the competition were all important to her, and, although she could have kicked herself for letting her anger getting the better of her in class, she really didn't see that there was anything wrong in her treatment of Delia. The girl had made a terrible mistake, and, in Millicent's view, she had thoroughly earned a good scolding.

Pam spoke to her in the common-room that evening, saying rather scornfully, 'Not the kind of behaviour one expects from a fifth former, Millicent. It is quite bad enough that you were working on your music, instead of concentrating on your French, but that little outburst of yours was simply disgraceful.'

Millicent turned red, and, becoming defensive, said, 'I don't see that there is any need for you to tick me off in front of the whole form, Pam.'

'Well, you yelled at Delia in front of all of us,' said Pam, quite reasonably. 'I really don't see the difference. And I think that you owe her an apology.'

'I shan't apologise!' said Millicent, growing even redder. 'Delia is an idiot.'

Bonnie, standing next to Delia, saw that the girl

looked close to tears, and pursed her lips. Suddenly she went across to her work-basket and picked up the pennants she had been working on. She had completed two, but the others were half-finished, and she walked across to Millicent, thrusting them at her.

'Here you are!' she said. 'You can finish them off yourself.'

Millicent looked simply flabbergasted, her mouth opening and closing, and she stammered, 'But, Bonnie, I can't sew! You know that I can't! You promised that you would do this for me.'

'Well, I've changed my mind,' said Bonnie, her little nose wrinkling in distaste. 'I don't like the way that you spoke to Delia, and I don't like you!'

Millicent, who had always thought of Bonnie as a rather weak, childish character, looked most taken aback, while the others watched with grins on their faces. They knew that Bonnie had a very obstinate streak in her nature, and unless Millicent made amends she would not back down.

Millicent looked at the faces around her, some of them scornful, some of them grinning at her discomfort. Gillian was looking at her as if she didn't like her very much at all, while June had a triumphant little smirk on her face. Suddenly Millicent realised that, if she refused to apologise to Delia, Gillian could decide to leave the orchestra altogether, and she would lose her best violinist. If she made the apology sound sincere enough, perhaps Bonnie would also reconsider, and finish making the pennants.

So Millicent swallowed her pride, and, trying to sound as sincere as possible, said, 'You are all absolutely right, I have been very unfair to Delia. I so badly want the orchestra to perform perfectly that I sometimes get carried away.'

Then she stepped towards Delia, holding out her hand, and said, 'Please accept my apology, Delia, old girl.'

Delia, who bore no malice and just felt relieved to be forgiven, seized Millicent's hand at once, and said, 'Of course I accept your apology, Millicent. And I hope that you will accept mine for being so stupid and forgetful during rehearsal.'

'What an ass Delia is!' whispered June to Freddie. 'It won't hurt Millicent to humble herself for once, and admit that she is in the wrong. But Delia has to go and apologise too and spoil it!'

Millicent, although she didn't feel like it at all, smiled brightly, then looked round at the others, saying contritely, 'I am sorry that my behaviour in Mam'zelle's class disgraced the form. You may be sure that it won't happen again.'

'Apology accepted,' said Pam. 'Now let's say no more about it.'

So the fifth formers went back to their various activities, and Bonnie took back the pile of sewing, which Millicent had placed on a chair.

'As you have apologised to Delia, I shall carry on making the pennants,' she said graciously. 'But my services are only on loan to you, Millicent, and a repeat of such behaviour means that I shall refuse to carry on sewing the pennants. And next time I shan't give you another chance.'

Chastened, Millicent went and sat alone in a corner, to read the French poem that Mam'zelle had given her as a punishment. She would much rather have been working at her music, but Millicent was well aware that she had had a lucky escape today, and didn't want to push Mam'zelle too far, in case she sent her to the Head.

Rather reluctantly, the girl decided that she had better start to pay attention in class, for she needed to devote all of her free time to the orchestra. And if she kept earning beastly punishments like this, she wouldn't *have* any free time.

'Gillian!' June called out suddenly. 'I'm organising a tennis practice for the fifth and sixth formers on Saturday afternoon. You'll come, won't you?'

'You bet!' answered Gillian, with enthusiasm.

The others often marvelled at Gillian's seemingly boundless energy, for she managed to fit in her orchestra rehearsals and tennis practice – not to mention lessons and prep – without feeling at all worn out.

'I don't know how you do it!' Nora said to her now. 'Honestly, Gillian, it makes me tired just to look at you sometimes.'

'That's because you're lazy,' June teased. 'But Gillian knows that good, hard practice brings rewards. Freddie, I want you there on Saturday, too, my girl. And you two, Felicity and Susan.'

Millicent looked up from her poem, a frown on her face, and said, 'Just a minute! June, Gillian can't possibly play tennis on Saturday afternoon, for I was planning to schedule another orchestra rehearsal then.'

'Hard luck,' said June, with an unsympathetic shrug. 'I got in first, so I'm afraid there's not an awful lot you can do about it.'

Millicent felt her temper rising, but, as she was already in the fifth form's bad books, she tried to speak calmly, saying, 'Gillian can play tennis at any time, but I don't have many opportunities to get the orchestra together as a whole.'

'My dear Millicent, I'm afraid that really isn't my problem,' said June coolly. 'If Gillian wishes to be on one of the teams, which she assures me she does, it is vital that she attends practice so that I can compare her standard of play with the others.'

Millicent's air of calm was fast deserting her, but at that moment Julie interrupted, to say, 'I shouldn't bother arguing about it, Millicent, for the sixth form has already booked the hall on Saturday afternoon. They are holding some sort of debate.'

'Well, that would seem to settle that, then!' said June, quite unable to keep the note of triumph out of her voice. She added kindly, 'Never mind, Millicent, perhaps you can book the hall for Sunday, instead.'

Scowling angrily at June, Millicent flung down her book, her good intentions of learning the French poem vanishing. The orchestra simply *had* to rehearse this weekend, especially after their poor showing yesterday, and all that mattered to her now was that she booked the hall for Sunday afternoon.

'Well!' said Susan, as Millicent rushed out of the room. 'It seems as if you are in for a jolly busy weekend, Gillian. What with tennis on Saturday and music on Sunday!'

'I shall have no free time at all,' Gillian realised suddenly. 'I wanted to do some shopping, for I need some new shoelaces, and I so wanted to buy some chocolate, but I shan't have time now. And I wanted to write some letters to my family and friends at home, too.'

'Well, Gillian,' said Nora. 'I can't help you with your letters, I'm afraid, but Pam and I are planning on going into the town on Saturday, so we can easily get you the things you want.'

'Thanks,' said Gillian gratefully. 'That's most awfully kind of you.'

But she had been looking forward to visiting the little shops in town herself. And it still didn't solve the problem of how she was to find the time to write her letters home. For the first time, Gillian began to wonder if she had bitten off more than she could chew!

6

The missing notebook

Saturday was a blisteringly hot day, and those fifth formers who were taking part in the tennis practice groaned.

'We shall all be like limp rags by the time we are finished,' complained Freddie.

But June wasn't to be deterred, and said, 'I'll ask Cook if we can have some jugs of lemonade to take down to the courts with us. That will refresh us in between games.'

So at two o'clock sharp, the girls trooped down to the tennis courts to begin their practice. Felicity and Susan played doubles against Gillian and Freddie, which June watched with a critical eye, before going off to play singles with one of the sixth formers.

Freddie wasn't quite as good a player as Felicity or Susan, for her tennis could be a little erratic. But Gillian more than made up for her faults, running all over the court and chasing every ball. Despite their best efforts, Felicity and Susan were beaten, and, afterwards, the four girls sat on the grass drinking lemonade as they watched June playing the sixth-form girl. The big sixth former was obviously suffering from the heat and tiring badly, but June looked as cool as a cucumber, her movements agile and nimble.

'June's jolly good, isn't she?' remarked Gillian. 'It's no wonder that she was made games captain, for she is so strong and determined.'

'You're not so bad yourself,' said Felicity. 'I think that you and June are pretty evenly matched.'

'I seem to tire more easily than June,' said Gillian, whose normally pale complexion had turned pink from the heat. 'I felt full of beans when we began playing, but by the end I felt as if I had been run ragged.'

'Well, I'm not surprised,' said Freddie, sipping her lemonade. 'I was off my game today, and you had to make up for me.'

'Are you sure that you aren't overdoing things, Gillian?' asked Susan, concerned. 'You've taken an awful lot on, agreeing to be part of the orchestra *and* a member of the tennis team.'

'I shall be fine,' said Gillian, putting a hand to her mouth to stifle a yawn. 'It's just that the heat has exhausted me today. I said that I could do both, and I intend to stick by my word.'

June, coming off court after running rings around the sixth-form girl, joined the others on the grass and poured herself a glass of lemonade.

'Just what I needed,' she said, after taking a long gulp. 'Gillian, you played marvellously, and I have decided that you, Elsie Horton of the sixth and me are going to be our singles players for the upper-school team against Summerfield Hall. Felicity and Susan, I would like you to play doubles. And Freddie …'

'Don't tell me,' said Freddie, with an air of gloom. 'I'm the reserve.'

'Sorry, old thing,' said June, giving her a wry smile. 'But, as games captain, I simply must pick the best players. You don't really mind, do you?'

Freddie didn't, for although she would have loved a place on the team, she knew only too well that her play was erratic, and June would have been a poor captain if she had chosen the girl over better players, simply because she was her friend.

'Of course not,' she said. 'At least I get a day out and a ride on the team bus, if we are playing at another school.'

Satisfied that Freddie was not upset, June was in a very good mood indeed. She now had just the team she wanted, as far as the upper school was concerned, and she had a very good idea who she was going to pick for the lower-school team too. Everything was falling neatly into place!

Millicent, meanwhile, was far from happy, for she had lost her notebook. The girl still did not realise that Gillian had picked it up, and had assumed that it must have fallen into her open satchel while she was distracted by Mam'zelle. But Millicent had turned out her satchel and it was nowhere to be seen.

Millicent had searched through her desk, and looked in the common-room, too, but the book seemed to have vanished into thin air. Scratching her head, Millicent decided that she might as well give up, for she was never going to find the notebook. Perhaps it was just as well that Delia hadn't made many notes, after all, for they would have been lost. Millicent made up her mind that she would get a new notebook, and this time she would jot down her own notes, instead of trusting the job to that foolish Delia.

Someone else who wanted to get hold of the notebook was Delia, for the girl didn't want Millicent spotting her 'silly little rhyme', as she thought of it, and making fun of it, perhaps in front of the others.

So, quite unaware that the book was in Gillian's possession, Delia thought that Millicent still had it, and went in search of it.

She passed Millicent on her way to the common-room, and noticed that the girl was carrying her purse, but didn't have her satchel with her. Delia's heart leapt. Was it possible that Millicent had left her bag unattended in the common-room?

Millicent had, and, what was more, no one was about, for most of the girls were outside enjoying the fine day.

The bag was on an armchair, and Delia bent over it, looking over her shoulder every so often, as she rifled through it. The girl had no intention of stealing the book, for all that she wanted was to tear out that one page.

But her search was fruitless, and, just as she was fastening the satchel up again, Delia heard a noise behind her, and turned to see Julie and Lucy in the doorway. Both girls had just been enjoying a ride, and they were looking forward to a quiet sit-down now.

'Hello, Delia,' said Lucy. Then she frowned. 'Isn't that Millicent's bag?'

Delia wasn't noted for her quick thinking, and she flushed and stammered, as she said, 'Er – yes, that's right. I – I noticed that it had come undone, and thought that something might fall out.'

And, with that, she pushed past the two girls and made her way down the corridor, her face a fiery red.

'Well!' said Julie, astonished. 'What do you make of that?'

'Delia certainly seemed flustered, didn't she?' said Lucy. 'I say, Julie, you don't think that she was up to no good, do you?'

'Stealing, you mean?' gasped Julie. 'Surely not! Why, Delia has always seemed a very decent sort to me.'

'Yes, to me, too,' said Lucy. 'But you can't deny that her behaviour was awfully suspicious.'

'I suppose it was,' said Julie, biting her lip. 'But here comes Millicent. She will be able to tell us if anything is missing from her bag. I say, Millicent! Have a look in your bag, and tell us if anything has been taken.'

Startled, Millicent said, 'Why? What has happened?'

'Well, we caught someone messing around with it,' said Lucy. 'So you had better check it.'

'Well, if anyone was after anything in my satchel, I suppose it would be my purse,' said Millicent. 'And I had that with me, for I had just been to ask Pam and Nora if they could get me a notebook while they were in town. Still, I suppose I had better make sure nothing is missing.'

Quickly, Millicent opened the bag and went through it. At last, she said, 'No, everything is here. The only thing I can't find is my notebook, but that went missing several days ago. That's why I asked Pam and Nora to get me a new one.'

Julie and Lucy both felt very relieved, until Millicent asked, 'Who was the girl that you caught meddling with it?'

The two girls exchanged glances. Neither of them wanted to mention Delia's name, especially as it looked as if she hadn't taken anything, after all, so Julie said, 'I didn't get a good look at her, did you, Lucy? She ran out past us as soon as she knew we had spotted her.'

'That's right,' said Lucy. 'She looked as if she could have been a first or second former.'

'Well, of all the nerve!' gasped Millicent. 'The cheek of those kids! Well, I'll jolly well make sure I don't leave my satchel lying around again.'

'Phew!' said Lucy, flopping down into a chair, as Millicent went out again. 'That was close. Thank goodness we found out that Delia wasn't trying to take anything, after all.'

'Well, we can't be too sure about that, Lucy,' said Julie, looking thoughtful. 'Perhaps she was after Millicent's purse. But Millicent had the purse with her, so if Delia *is* a thief, it may be that she was just out of luck.'

Gillian was quite unaware of all the drama that was taking place surrounding the notebook. The girl had completely forgotten that she had ever picked it up, and it lay discarded now, in the bottom of her satchel. Her fingers even brushed against it when she reached in her bag for her comb, in the changing-room, after tennis. But Gillian did not notice, nor remember that the book was there, as she went into tea with the others.

Pam and Nora weren't there, as the two of them had decided to have tea in town, a privilege that the two top forms were allowed.

'I bet they've gone to that nice little tea-shop,' said Felicity, rather enviously. 'The one that does the lovely little sandwiches, and those delicious chocolate cakes.'

'Well, we are not doing too badly,' said Susan, spreading apricot jam thickly on to a slice of bread and butter. 'This jam is super. And we've got coffee instead of tea, which makes a pleasant change.'

'I could do with a cup of coffee to keep me awake,' said Gillian, putting her hand up to her mouth to stifle a yawn. 'That game of tennis has quite worn me out.'

Millicent overheard this, and she said rather sharply, 'I do hope you're not going to be too tired to concentrate on the rehearsal tomorrow, Gillian. As you are the best violinist, you have quite a complicated solo to learn.'

'I shan't let you down,' said Gillian stiffly, nettled by Millicent's tone. 'I have been practising the solo all week.'

'That's true,' said Lucy. 'Julie and I passed one of the music-rooms yesterday afternoon, and there was old Gillian scraping away at her violin for all she was worth. I must say, it sounded jolly good. Did you really write that yourself, Millicent?'

Trying not to look too pleased at this, Millicent answered, 'Of course.'

'Well, you're very talented,' said Julie. 'Anyone would think that it had been written by a *real* composer.'

The others laughed at this, and, much to their surprise, Millicent joined in. She quite understood what Julie meant, and she was pleased at the compliment, especially as she felt that most of the fifth formers didn't really like her very much.

'The whole piece took me simply ages, and it was so difficult that I almost gave up at times,' Millicent said. 'But once I had finished, and knew that I had created something worthwhile, it was worth all the hard work. Sometimes I think that I enjoy composing more than playing.'

Felicity looked at Millicent, and thought how different she was when she was talking honestly about something that she loved. Her face looked more open, and less intense, somehow, and her rather dramatic tone of voice was lighter.

'Have you always been musical?' she asked curiously.

'Oh yes, for music is in my blood, you know,' answered Millicent. 'My mother was a concert pianist, and she taught me how to play the piano when I was quite small. I took to it at once, and it was obvious even then that I had a gift.'

Suddenly the girl gave a rather self-conscious laugh, and said, 'That sounds awfully conceited, doesn't it, but I truly don't mean it to.'

'I suppose that you were a musical genius from the moment you could walk, too, Gillian?' said Susan.

'I would hardly call myself a genius,' said Gillian, with a grin. 'I can't play a variety of instruments, as Millicent can, and if someone asked me to compose a tune I wouldn't know where to start. I do so love playing my violin though.'

That was the difference between the two girls, thought Felicity. As far as Millicent was concerned, music was the be all and end all. But she took it so very seriously that she didn't seem to get a great deal of pleasure from it. Gillian, however, took great joy in her music, and this made her performances very special, for everyone listening felt her enthusiasm and shared in it.

Pam and Nora returned to school soon after the others had left the tea-table, and joined them in the common-room.

'Hallo, everyone!' called out Pam. 'My word, we've had a super time. A spot of shopping, then a most marvellous tea.'

'Gillian, I have your shoelaces here,' said Nora, rummaging in her bag. 'And the chocolate you asked for.'

'And here is your book, Millicent,' said Pam, handing the girl a notebook identical to the one she had mislaid.

'Thanks,' said Millicent. She looked round the room to see if Delia was there, and, seeing that she was absent, said, 'I shan't trust that idiot of a Delia to make notes in it though. I shall do it myself from now on.'

'Oh, Delia's not a bad sort,' said Susan. 'She means well.'

Julie and Lucy heard this, and exchanged glances.

'I wonder what Susan would think if she knew that we had caught Delia looking in Millicent's bag earlier,' murmured Julie.

'You're not going to tell her, are you?' whispered Lucy, looking rather alarmed. 'I mean to say, we have no proof that Delia was doing anything wrong. It may have been just as she said, and she was merely fastening the bag up.'

'I shan't say anything to Susan, or anyone else, yet,' said Julie. 'But I shall be keeping an eye on Delia.'

Delia came into the common-room just then, and at once she spotted the notebook in Millicent's hand. Of course, Delia wasn't to know that it was a brand-new one, and she assumed that it was the one that contained her rhyme. Millicent slipped the book into the pocket of her school dress, and Delia's mind began to race. If only there was a way of getting hold of it for a moment. It would only take a matter of seconds to find the page with her scribbled words on and tear it out.

Delia's chance came at bedtime that evening. Millicent had changed into her pyjamas and, while she was in the bathroom brushing her teeth, Pam noticed that she had carelessly flung her dress on the bed.

'I do hope that Millicent intends to hang her dress up,' said Pam. 'She's awfully untidy, and it makes things unpleasant for the rest of us if we have to sleep in a messy room.'

'I'll hang it up for her,' offered Delia, picking the dress

up. As she smoothed it down, she could feel the notebook, still in the pocket, and her heart leapt. Delia was just about to slip her hand into the pocket, when she realised that Julie was watching her, an odd expression on her face.

Quickly, Delia moved her hand away, her face turning red, as she realised that she must look most suspicious.

'Lucy!' said Julie in a low voice. 'Did you see that?'

But Lucy, who had been deep in conversation with Freddie, hadn't seen a thing.

'Well, Delia offered to hang Millicent's dress up for her,' explained Julie. 'And she was just about to put her hand in the pocket, until she saw me watching her and stopped.'

'Heavens!' said Lucy, in dismay. 'Her behaviour is awfully strange, I must say, but no one in the form has had anything stolen, so we can't really tackle her about it. All that we can do is keep watching her.'

Delia had another opportunity to feel in the pocket of Millicent's dress the following day, when the girl left her school dress lying on the bed again. This time she was alone in the dormitory, and she seized her chance. But, to Delia's dismay, the book was no longer there. Millicent must have moved it elsewhere, for safe-keeping. How annoying! Perhaps it was in Millicent's desk? As it was Sunday, there were no lessons that day, so Delia thought that it would be a perfect opportunity to slip into the class-room unnoticed, and take a peek.

But her luck was well and truly out, for she was caught

in the act yet again – this time by Bonnie and Amy.

Cautiously, Delia lifted the lid and peered in, moving things very carefully and putting them back in exactly the same place, so that Millicent would not notice that someone had been in there. But there was no sign of the elusive notebook. Of course, Delia thought suddenly, there was a rehearsal later today, so Millicent was bound to have the notebook on her, probably in her bag. Which meant that she, Delia, had absolutely no chance of getting her hands on it until the rehearsal was over. She put the lid down, then gave a terrific start. For Amy and Bonnie had entered the class-room, and were giving her very strange looks indeed!

'W-what are you doing here?' she stammered.

'I wanted a book from my desk,' said Amy coldly. 'And what exactly are you doing, Delia?'

'I er – I thought I heard a knocking sound,' she said to the two girls, her cheeks beginning to burn. 'And it seemed to be coming from inside Millicent's desk.'

'Well, I can't hear anything,' said Bonnie, thinking Delia's explanation very lame indeed. 'Did you find anything in there?'

'No, nothing at all,' said Delia, with a nervous little laugh. 'I daresay my ears were playing tricks on me.'

'I daresay,' said Amy, with a sniff. 'But I must tell you, Delia, that it really isn't the done thing to go poking around in another girl's desk without her permission, you know.'

'Yes, I realise that,' said poor Delia, turning even

redder. 'Normally I wouldn't think of doing such a thing. It's just that ...'

'You thought you heard a knocking sound,' Bonnie said, as Delia's voice tailed off.

Bonnie and Amy exchanged meaningful glances. Neither of them believed Delia's story for a moment, and thought that her manner had been very suspicious. And both of them would dearly have liked to know what she was really up to.

The term goes on

The orchestra's rehearsal that afternoon went very well indeed. There were still odd mistakes, and the occasional wrong note, but on the whole the girls played beautifully. There was only one girl who wasn't up to the standard of the others, and, strangely enough, that girl was Gillian.

Although she had spent a great deal of time rehearsing her violin solo in one of the little music-rooms, she played badly, and without her usual passion.

But Millicent, for once, held her tongue and did not scold. She noticed that Gillian looked rather pale and tired, and guessed that the girl was finding it a strain attending both the frequent tennis practices and practising her music. It was on the tip of her tongue to tell Gillian that she would have to choose between the two. But then, thought Millicent, the girl might choose tennis, and that would leave her without anyone to play the violin solo. No doubt one of the others could learn it, but Gillian was far and away the best violinist in the school, and Millicent didn't want to lose her.

But her decision to let the girl off lightly did not go down well with the rest of the orchestra.

'I was scolded for playing one wrong note,' grumbled Anne. 'And when poor Janet lost her place, I quite thought that Millicent was going to throw the baton at her!'

'Yes, but she didn't say a word to Gillian, and she played dreadfully,' said Jessie from East Tower. 'It's out-and-out favouritism.'

Millicent, quite unaware of the ill-feeling brewing, rapped sharply on her music stand with her baton, and said, 'Well, most of you played a little better today, but you are still not up to competition standard. Please spend as much time as you can practising your parts, particularly those of you with solos. I think that from now I shall hold two rehearsals a week, instead of one, otherwise we shall never be ready.'

There were groans at this, and some of the girls muttered under their breath.

'I wish that I had never joined the beastly orchestra,' said Janet, with a scowl. 'I thought that it would be fun, but this is too much like hard work.'

'It wouldn't be so bad if we got a word of praise now and again,' said Jessie. 'Millicent should take a leaf out of June's book. June works her tennis players hard, but she encourages them with plenty of praise, and knows how to get the best out of them.'

June certainly did. Helped by Felicity and Susan, she was coaching some of the first and second formers that afternoon, and it was clear that the youngsters simply adored her.

'Becoming games captain has really brought out a softer side in June,' said Felicity, watching with approval as the girl sat on the grass talking to some of the younger girls.

'I was a little afraid that the power might go to her head,' said Susan. 'But it hasn't at all, I'm pleased to say.'

Just then, June got up and came over to the two girls, and said, 'I think it's time that we decided who to put into the lower-school team.'

'Young Hannah must certainly play,' said Felicity. 'She has worked so hard, and come on in leaps and bounds.'

'I agree,' said June. 'So has little Christine. She and Dorothy play very well together, so I think that we should pick them for the doubles.'

'Barbara and Kathleen of the first form are very good too,' put in Susan. 'Perhaps we could choose one of them to play singles, and the other as reserve.'

So it was agreed that Kathleen would be in the team and Barbara would be reserve, and the fifth formers went across to the younger girls to give them the news.

There were whoops and yells from those who had been chosen, while the others cheered and clapped them on the back. Some of those who hadn't got a place on the team looked disappointed, but June noticed this and said, 'Just because you haven't been chosen this time doesn't mean that you will *never* play for the team. You have all tried your best and I feel very proud of you, and want you to keep up your practice. Don't forget that I shall be arranging some exhibition matches for half-term, and I shall need some good players for those.'

This cheered the disappointed girls enormously. Being chosen for the half-term matches wasn't *quite* as good as playing for the school, but a tremendous honour, all the same.

The fifth formers bumped into Gillian, who had just come out of rehearsal, as they went back into the school, but the girl seemed quite preoccupied and barely noticed them, until Susan said, 'What's up, Gillian? Have you sent us all to Coventry, or something?'

Gillian blinked, then said, 'Awfully sorry, Susan. I didn't mean to ignore you, but I was in a world of my own.'

'Are you quite all right?' said Felicity, noticing how pale and strained the girl looked.

'Of course,' said Gillian, pinning a bright smile to her face. 'Just a little tired, that's all. I didn't sleep very well last night, but I'm sure that I'll make up for it tonight, and I shall be as right as rain tomorrow.'

'Why don't you go for a walk outside?' suggested June. 'That will blow the cobwebs away. It's a glorious day, and if you get some fresh air that will help you to sleep well tonight.'

'Later, perhaps,' said Gillian. 'I must go and practise my solo first, for I do so want it to be perfect.'

'She is doing far too much, and tiring herself out,' said Felicity, as the girl walked away. 'If she carries on like this, June, she won't be fit to play tennis *or* be part of the orchestra.'

'Well, it was her own decision to do both,' said June.

'I would be more than happy if she decided to leave the orchestra and concentrate on her tennis.'

But Felicity was far from happy, and she sought out Pam, the calm, sensible head of the form. Pam listened to what Felicity had to say, an unusually serious expression on her face, and, at last, she said, 'I'm going to tackle Gillian about this business. Her health and her work are both going to suffer if she carries on as she is.'

'Well, you will probably find her in one of the music-rooms,' said Felicity. 'She seems to spend most of her time in there, or on the tennis-courts.'

So Pam went off to find Gillian, and soon heard the sound of a violin coming from one of the rooms. But surely that couldn't be Gillian, for the player seemed uncertain and hesitant, with many wrong notes coming from the instrument! Quietly, Pam pushed open the door, and, much to her surprise, discovered that the violinist *was* Gillian. She hadn't heard Pam come in, and there was a frown of intense concentration on her face as she scraped the bow across the strings. Pam, watching her, thought how different she looked from the joyous, music-loving girl who had played for them in the common-room. Now Gillian looked as if she was undertaking a rather unpleasant chore.

Pam gave a little cough and stepped into the room.

Gillian immediately looked up, her bow becoming still, and said, 'Hallo, Pam. Did you want me? Only I'm rather busy, you see, for I simply must practise this solo.'

'I'd like to talk to you, Gillian,' said Pam, the serious

expression on her face so different from her usual calm, serene one that Gillian felt quite alarmed.

'I haven't done anything wrong, have I?' asked Gillian, rather anxiously.

'No, you haven't done anything wrong,' answered Pam, coming further into the room. 'But I am very worried about you, and so are some of the others.'

'Really?' said Gillian, looking most astonished. 'Well, I don't know why you should be, Pam.'

'The thing is, Gillian, that we feel you are overdoing things a bit, what with all your tennis practice and the orchestra rehearsals,' said Pam. 'You look awfully tired, and when I watched you playing just then, it seemed to me that you weren't enjoying it at all.'

'Nonsense, Pam!' said Gillian, giving a little laugh, which, to Pam's ears, sounded rather strained. 'I adore both music and tennis, so by choosing to play in the team and the orchestra, I really am having the best of both worlds. If I looked a little tense when I was playing, it's because this violin solo is awfully difficult.'

'Perhaps you are finding it difficult because you're exhausted,' suggested Pam.

'I am a little tired,' admitted Gillian.

'Well, for goodness' sake, forget about both your music and your tennis for a bit and just relax, and read a book or something.'

Gillian really didn't want to do this, for she was determined to master her solo before the next rehearsal, and couldn't afford to waste any time. But she liked the kind-hearted Pam, and could see that the girl genuinely had her best interests at heart. Besides, thought Gillian, if she went against Pam now, and insisted on carrying on with her practice, the head-girl would worry about her even more and keep a close watch on her, and perhaps even talk June or Millicent into dropping her. That would never do, for although Gillian really was finding it far more of a strain than she had anticipated to fit in both tennis and music, she was determined to stick to her word. So she smiled at Pam, began to put her violin in her case, and said, 'Perhaps you're right, and I do need a break. I'll go and sit in the sun and read my book for a while.'

So Pam went off, happy that she had talked some sense into Gillian. The head-girl wasn't to know that Gillian only stayed outside for about ten minutes, then, as soon as she was sure that the coast was clear, sneaked back up to the music-room to play her violin once more!

The other new girl, Delia, was at a bit of a loose end, meanwhile, and rather bored. She was still quite desperate to get her hands on Millicent's notebook, but the girl had it with her in the common-room and was writing something down in it. Delia had sat and watched her for a while, hoping that Millicent might go away and leave it lying around. Then she, Delia, would be able to whip out that silly rhyme she had written and destroy it, before Millicent had the chance to ridicule her.

But Millicent did not move, continuing to scribble away in the notebook, and soon she realised that Delia was watching her and became exasperated.

'Why do you keep staring at me all the time?' she snapped. 'It's most annoying. Don't you have anything better to do?'

Delia didn't answer, for the truth was that she *didn't* have anything to do. She liked the fifth formers, and most of them seemed to like her, but Delia had no particular friend of her own, so she tended to get a little left out sometimes. Millicent and Gillian didn't have special friends either, but both of them had interests and activities to occupy their time, where poor Delia had nothing.

Fortunately, Felicity and Susan came into the common-room in time to overhear Millicent's remarks. Felicity saw Delia's rather downcast expression, and said kindly, 'I say, Delia, why not come for a walk with Susan and me? We were thinking of popping over to see Bill and Clarissa.'

Delia cheered up at this, and asked curiously, 'Who are Bill and Clarissa?'

'They are two old girls who run a riding school not very far from here,' explained Susan. 'They were in the same form as Felicity's older sister, Darrell.'

'Yes, they're jolly good sorts,' said Felicity. 'Do come, Delia, for we haven't had a chance to introduce you to them yet.'

It was very pleasant to feel wanted, so Delia agreed at once, and went off happily with Felicity and Susan.

Bill and Clarissa were very pleased to see the three

girls, and made them welcome. Then they had a fine time watching some children having riding-lessons and petting all the horses. Delia was a little nervous of them at first, but once she realised they weren't going to bite her, or kick out at her, she soon relaxed. Felicity and Susan were good company, and she liked the two older girls, Bill and Clarissa, and Delia enjoyed herself very much indeed.

By the time they made their way back to Malory Towers, the girl felt in such high spirits that she began to hum cheerfully to herself. The tune that she hummed was Gillian's violin solo from 'Summer Serenade' and, almost without realising it, Delia found herself softly singing the words that she had written to accompany it.

'What is that song you're singing, Delia?' asked Felicity curiously. 'I don't think that I've heard it before.'

Delia could have kicked herself, for she hadn't realised that Felicity and Susan had stopped talking and were listening to her silly little song. Of course, Delia didn't want to admit that she had written the words herself, for the others were sure to laugh at her, so she said, 'I don't know. It must have been something that I heard on the radio and it just got stuck in my head.'

'I shall have to listen out for it,' said Felicity. 'It's awfully good.'

'Yes,' agreed Susan. 'It really captures the spirit of summer, somehow.'

Another girl might have felt proud at this, but not Delia, who hadn't come in for a great deal of praise in her life. She merely thought that the two girls were captivated by the tune, rather than the words, and that was to Millicent's credit.

'Sing a little more – louder, this time,' said Felicity, but Delia turned red and shook her head, saying, 'I can't remember any more of the words. And I'm sure that my singing voice isn't very pleasant to listen to. Let's talk instead. I say, it's coming up to half-term soon, isn't it? Won't that be fun?'

Felicity and Susan accepted the change of subject, Susan saying, 'I simply can't wait! Daddy may not be able to come, but Mother will. She has promised to take me to a restaurant for a slap-up meal.'

'My parents are both coming,' said Felicity, happily. 'I'm so looking forward to seeing them again. How about you, Delia? Will your people be coming?'

'I doubt if my aunt will bother,' said Delia. 'Not that I particularly want to see her anyway, or my cousins. My father will be on leave from his ship, though, so he is coming.'

Felicity and Susan noticed how Delia's eyes shone when she spoke of her father, and knew that she must love him very much.

'It must be awfully difficult for you,' said Felicity, earnestly. 'Having to live away from your father most of the time.'

'Yes, but he has to earn a living,' said Delia with a sigh. Then she brightened, and added, 'And it does make the times that we are together so much more special.

When he comes home on leave Father likes to spend as much time as possible with me, and we do so much together.'

'Does he know that you are unhappy at your aunt's?' asked Felicity curiously.

Delia shook her head firmly, and said, 'No, for it would only worry him if he knew, and then he wouldn't be able to concentrate on his job. Besides, there's no point in making a big fuss about it, for as long as Father is at sea there really isn't any alternative. And I suppose things could be worse. It's not as if my aunt ill-treats me, or starves me, or anything like that. It's just that I know she would rather I wasn't there, and my cousins feel the same.'

Felicity and Susan said nothing, but both of them felt rather sorry for Delia. They admired her, too, for having the strength of character to accept her situation without complaining, for the sake of the father she adored.

'I think that's jolly sensible of you, Delia,' said Felicity. 'And I don't suppose that your father will be at sea forever, so it will all be worth it in the end.'

'No, he plans to find a job on shore in a year or so,' said Delia. 'Then I shall be able to live with him all the time. In the meantime, I can't tell you how happy I am to be at Malory Towers, for it is much nicer than going to day school with my horrid cousins. The only thing I miss is not having a friend of my own.'

'Well, you're quite welcome to tag along with Felicity and me sometimes,' said Susan. 'Though I quite understand what you mean, for it is nice to have a special friend of your own.'

'Why don't you try to pal up with Gillian, or Millicent?' suggested Felicity. 'They are both on their own as well.'

'I don't think that Millicent feels very friendly towards me since I forgot to take notes at her rehearsal,' said Delia ruefully. 'And Gillian is always so busy that she doesn't seem to have time for any real friendships.'

'Well, perhaps she should make time,' said Felicity. 'I think that it would do her good to think about something besides her music and her tennis.'

'Felicity is quite right,' said Susan. 'Why don't you try and make friends with her, Delia, and take her out of herself a bit? It would do both of you the world of good.'

'All right, then, I shall!' said Delia, feeling a lot more cheerful suddenly. 'Of course, I don't know if it will work, or if Gillian will even *want* to be friends with me, but I shall certainly try.'

8

A new friendship

Delia was as good as her word, and, the following afternoon, when Gillian was looking for someone to practise her serve on, she seized the opportunity.

'Felicity and Susan are both helping June to coach the youngsters, and Freddie has promised to play with Helen Jones of the fourth form,' complained Gillian. 'Now what am I to do, for I do so need to practise.'

'Will I do?' asked Delia. 'I probably shan't return many of your serves, for I'm hopeless at tennis, but you are very welcome to practise on me.'

Gillian, who knew that Delia always tried to avoid playing tennis because she was afraid of showing herself up, felt very grateful indeed, and said, 'Why, thank you, Delia. Come on, let's go and get changed, and bag a court.'

In fact, Delia did manage to return a few of the other girl's serves, for Gillian was off her game a little that day.

Delia, however, had no idea of this, and began to feel that she wasn't quite as bad at tennis as she had always thought.

'Well!' she exclaimed, as she and Gillian got changed afterwards. 'Who would have thought that I could get so many of your serves back?'

Delia sounded so pleased with herself that Gillian didn't have the heart to tell her the truth. Instead, she forced a smile and said lightly, 'If you practise a little more, I daresay June will soon be giving my place on the team to you!'

Delia laughed at this, and said, 'I don't know about that. I say, Gillian, how about popping into town for a spot of tea? We can get a bus just along the road, and it would make a pleasant change from school tea.'

Gillian hesitated. She badly wanted to get in half an hour's violin practice before tea, and there wouldn't be time if they were to catch the bus.

She said as much to Delia, adding, 'Besides, I'm broke. I had to buy a birthday present for Mother last week, and I'm down to my last few pence.'

'My treat,' said Delia. 'I'm pretty well off at the moment.'

Gillian looked surprised at this, for Delia was one of the girls who had very little money. It wasn't that her father was poor, for he regularly sent money to Delia's aunt for her. But her aunt was sometimes a little forgetful about sending it on to Delia, which meant that the girl had very little to spend on herself.

'My grandmother sent me a nice, big postal order the other day,' Delia said now. 'And it's no fun going off and having tea on my own, so I'd be jolly grateful if you would come with me.'

The expression in Delia's eyes reminded Gillian of a friendly, eager-to-please puppy, and somehow she couldn't bring herself to snub the girl. Instead, she slipped her arm through Delia's, and said, 'Nonsense! I'm the one who should be grateful to you for such a treat. Thanks, Delia.'

Delia turned quite red with pleasure, and the two girls went off together to catch the bus.

Pam noticed that they were missing at tea-time, and said with a frown, 'If Gillian is missing her tea so that she can practise the violin, or play tennis, I shall be cross with her.'

'I think that she's gone out with Delia,' said Julie. 'Lucy and I saw them waiting at the bus stop along the road when we came back from our ride earlier.'

Felicity and Susan exchanged pleased glances. It seemed that Delia had taken their advice and was going out of her way to befriend Gillian.

'It will be jolly good for both of them,' said Felicity. 'I really hope that they hit it off.'

'And that will only leave Millicent without a friend of her own,' said Susan. 'Although she doesn't seem to need one, for she is so wrapped up in her music.'

'Even Millicent must have times when she needs someone to talk to, and confide in,' said Felicity. 'But really, it's quite her own fault that she doesn't have one, for she isn't the easiest of people to get on with.'

Delia and Gillian, meanwhile, were getting along like a house on fire. For the first time in weeks, Gillian's head wasn't full of music scores or tennis shots, as she and Delia chattered away together. Delia really could be very funny at times, thought Gillian, as the two girls sat in the little tea shop feasting on the most delicious crumpets, dripping with melted butter, and little scones, warm from the oven, filled with jam and cream.

'Thank you so much for inviting me, Delia,' said Gillian, as the two of them finished their tea. 'I've had a super time and it has really taken me out of myself.'

'Well, I'm jolly glad to hear it,' said Delia a little gruffly, feeling very pleased that Gillian had enjoyed herself so much.

She took a five pound note out of her purse and got up to go and pay the bill, but as she did so, she knocked Gillian's bag on to the floor, sending the contents everywhere.

'Oh, dear!' she wailed. 'I'm so clumsy.'

'Don't worry,' laughed Gillian, as the two girls crouched down to pick everything up. 'Anyone can have an accident, and there's no harm done.'

There had been a bag of sweets in the bag, and they had rolled all over the floor, and as Gillian scrabbled around picking them up, Delia spotted something that made her give a little gasp. Millicent's notebook! But what on earth was it doing in Gillian's bag? There was no time to puzzle over that just now, though. While Gillian was looking the other way, Delia grabbed it and slipped it into her pocket, giving a sigh of relief. As soon as she had a moment to herself, she would tear out the page that she needed, then she would leave the book somewhere Millicent would be sure to find it.

Delia felt horribly guilty as she and Gillian made their way back to Malory Towers, for she was an honest girl and she didn't like being in possession of something that didn't belong to her. She simply couldn't think what Gillian had been doing with Millicent's notebook, but the sooner it was back in the hands of its rightful owner, the better.

Delia slipped up to the dormitory when she and Gillian got back to the school, relieved to find that it was empty. Swiftly she ripped out the page at the back, crumpling it up and stuffing it in one of her drawers. Then she placed the notebook on Millicent's bedside cabinet. No doubt Millicent would wonder how it had got there, but that couldn't be helped!

Gillian wasn't in the common-room when Delia joined the others, and the girl guessed that she must be shut away in one of the little music-rooms, playing her violin.

There was a low hum of noise in the common-room – nothing like the hubbub that the lower forms created, for the fifth formers would certainly have considered it beneath their dignity to make such a racket. Instead it was rather a pleasant, soothing noise, thought Delia, of girls in low-voiced, friendly conversation, while the radio played soft music in the background. Little did she know that the peace was about to be rudely shattered!

'I say, Millicent!' said Nora. 'I hate to ask, but are you able to let me have that five shillings I lent you the other day? I need to buy some new stockings, for even Matron agrees that the ones I have are beyond repair!'

Millicent looked up from the music score she had been working on, and said, 'Of course. Sorry, Nora, it completely slipped my mind, but you can have it back now.'

Millicent rummaged in her bag for her purse, then she gave a little cry. 'It's gone!' she said. 'My purse is gone.'

'It can't be,' said Susan. 'Check in your pockets.'

Millicent stood up and felt in her pockets, but the missing purse wasn't there. 'Blow!' she said, frowning. 'I had a few pounds in there, too, for my mother had just sent me some money.'

'Are you sure it's not in the dormitory?' said Felicity. 'Perhaps it's in your cabinet.'

Millicent ran upstairs to take a look, and was back within minutes.

'No purse, but I did find this,' said Millicent, brandishing the notebook that Delia had left on her cabinet earlier. 'I lost it several weeks ago, and now it has suddenly turned up again.'

'How queer!' said Pam, who had begun to feel rather uneasy. How she hoped that Millicent's purse would turn up, for if it didn't that might mean that there was a thief in the fifth form.

Delia turned very red when Millicent produced the notebook, and lowered her eyes, hoping that none of the others were looking in her direction, for she felt that she must look very guilty indeed.

But some of the girls *were* looking at her. Julie and

Lucy, who had caught Delia going through Millicent's bag, and Amy and Bonnie, who had seen her looking in the girl's desk, were watching her with suspicion. When Delia turned red and looked down, Amy and Bonnie exchanged meaningful glances, while Julie nudged Lucy and murmured, 'Just look at Delia's face! The picture of guilt.'

'Millicent, when did you have your purse last?' asked Pam, taking charge of the situation. 'Think carefully.'

Millicent thought, and said, 'I had it yesterday morning, for one of the sixth formers came round to collect for Miss Potts's birthday present, and I put a shilling in.'

'That's right,' said Bonnie. 'I saw you, and I remember that you put your purse in your bag afterwards.'

'So it could have been taken any time after that,' said Felicity. 'Millicent, was your bag out of your sight at any time?'

'Only when I went to bed,' said poor Millicent, who was looking very upset now. 'I left it here, in the common-room.'

'Oh, Millicent, how silly!' said Pam. 'You should always take it up to the dormitory with you.'

'I know,' said Millicent rather sheepishly. 'I usually do, but I simply forgot last night.'

'Well, I suppose there is still a chance that it will turn up somewhere,' said Felicity, trying to sound cheery, though she didn't feel very hopeful.

'Perhaps, but in the meantime I can't pay Nora back,'

said Millicent. 'I'm awfully sorry, Nora. I shall write to Mother, of course, and explain what has happened. She will send me some more money, and I shall give it to you as soon as I can, but I'm afraid that I won't get it for a while.'

'Don't worry about that,' said Nora. 'I'm only sorry that your purse has gone missing. And I shall be sorry when Matron sees me going around in holey stockings and gives me a row!'

The others laughed at that, and Pam said, 'I will lend you the money to buy some new stockings, Nora. We can't have you disgracing the fifth by wearing ragged ones.'

The girls began to talk about other things, for no one quite liked to mention the one thing that was on all their minds in front of everyone – the possibility that there was a thief in the fifth form.

Some of the girls discussed it among themselves, though, and Amy remarked to Bonnie, 'Things look black for Delia.'

'I suppose they do,' said Bonnie. 'She doesn't strike me as dishonest, I must say, though her behaviour was most peculiar the day we caught her in Millicent's desk.'

Julie and Lucy, standing nearby, overheard this, and Julie moved closer to Bonnie, saying in a low voice, 'What was that, Bonnie? Did I hear you say that you had caught Delia in Millicent's desk?'

'Yes,' said Bonnie. 'It looked as if she was searching for something.'

Lucy gave a low whistle, and said, 'Well, Julie and I

found her looking in Millicent's bag not very long ago. She came up with some tale to explain it away, but it wasn't very convincing.'

'How beastly that this should happen now, just as we are all looking forward to half-term next weekend,' said Julie, looking worried.

'Do you think that we should tell Pam that we suspect Delia?' asked Amy. 'As head-girl, she really ought to be informed, for she is the one who will have to decide what to do.'

'I think that we should wait until after half-term,' said Bonnie. 'Otherwise it will put an awful damper on what should be a happy time.'

'I agree,' said Lucy. 'Let's just keep it between the four of us for now. And we had better keep a careful eye on Delia in the meantime, and see if anyone else's belongings disappear.'

'I say!' said Julie, suddenly. 'Didn't Delia and Gillian have tea in town together this afternoon? It would be interesting to know where Delia found the money to pay her share, for she always seems to be broke.'

'Perhaps Gillian treated her,' suggested Bonnie.

'Well, we can ask her,' said Amy. 'Here she comes.'

Just then Gillian came into the common-room, looking nothing like the happy, carefree girl who had gone to tea with Delia that afternoon.

The strained expression was back on her face, and she looked very pale. But Julie, intent on finding out what she wanted to know, didn't even notice this, and called out, 'Hi, Gillian! Come here a moment, would you?'

Bonnie, knowing that Julie wasn't the most tactful of souls, stepped forward and said, 'Are you all right, Gillian? You look awfully tired.'

'I'm fine,' Gillian assured her brightly. 'Did you want something, Julie?'

Julie opened her mouth, but, once more, Bonnie forestalled her, saying, 'Well, it's no wonder that you're tired, with all the activities that you do. Going out for tea with Delia must have been a pleasant break for you.'

Julie, who had been rather put out by Bonnie pushing herself forward, suddenly realised what the girl was doing. She was leading up to the question tactfully, rather than being blunt, and perhaps causing offence. And, by using such tactics, she was likely to get a great deal more out of Gillian, thought Julie, staring at little Bonnie with admiration.

'Oh, yes, we had a marvellous time,' Gillian was saying now. 'And a super tea! I was so grateful to Delia for inviting me.'

'She's such a thoughtful girl,' said Bonnie, smiling sweetly at Gillian. 'So generous with her time.'

'And with her money,' said Gillian. 'I've spent all of my pocket money this week, so Delia treated me. Wasn't that kind of her?'

'It certainly was,' said Bonnie. 'Especially as poor Delia never seems to have very much money.'

'Well, it was jolly lucky for me that she had just received a postal order from her grandmother,' said

Gillian. 'Otherwise I shouldn't have had such a splendid treat.'

'Well done, Bonnie,' murmured Lucy, patting the girl on the back, as Gillian moved away. 'You handled that perfectly.'

'I should say!' agreed Julie. 'Why, you didn't even have to ask Gillian who had paid for tea, for she volunteered the information.'

'It was simply a question of leading her in the right direction,' said Bonnie modestly. 'And now we know the truth. Delia received some money from her grandmother.'

But the others weren't convinced, Julie saying darkly, 'Hmm. Well, I think it's rather a coincidence that Delia happens to be in funds just as Millicent's purse goes missing.'

'I agree,' said Amy. 'I shall certainly be keeping an eye on my belongings from now on.'

'And I shall be keeping an eye on Delia,' said Lucy. 'We *all* should. I know that we have agreed not to say anything to Pam and the others until after half-term, but that doesn't mean that we can't watch Delia, and make sure that she doesn't get the chance to steal anything else.'

'Well, we don't know for certain that Delia is the culprit,' said Bonnie, looking unusually grave. 'And I, for one, would like to make absolutely sure that we have our facts right before we start making accusations.'

'You're quite right, of course,' said Lucy. 'And I would

never dream of accusing Delia, or anyone else, for that matter, without proof. All I am saying is that it won't do any harm to watch her.'

'I suppose not,' said Bonnie. 'But we must be careful that Delia doesn't realise what we are up to, for if it turns out that she *is* the person who took Millicent's purse, we don't want to put her on her guard.'

Delia, meanwhile, quite unaware that she was under suspicion, was turning over some rather disturbing and unwelcome thoughts in her own mind. She was remembering how Millicent's notebook had been in Gillian's possession, and was wondering how the girl had come by it. Had Gillian taken it from Millicent's bag? And, if so, was it possible that the girl had taken the purse as well?

Delia felt very troubled indeed, for she liked Gillian very much, and the thought that the girl might be a thief was horrible. Delia had so enjoyed the time they had spent together, and had been secretly hoping that the two of them might become close friends. But, if Gillian turned out to be dishonest, that would be quite impossible.

Just then, Gillian herself came over and sat down next to Delia, a smile of genuine friendship on her rather white face. Delia was unable to stop herself smiling back and, as she did so, she realised something. If she wanted to be a true friend to Gillian, she had to be loyal and believe in her. And, looking into the girl's open, honest face, Delia's suspicions fell away. Of course Gillian wasn't a thief! Why, she just couldn't be, for surely she, Delia, couldn't possibly like her so much if she was dishonest.

Oddly enough, Millicent herself was the person who seemed least affected by the loss of her purse. She had quickly put it out of her mind, for an idea of how she could improve Gillian's violin solo had suddenly come to her, and she was now sitting at the big table working on her score. She had been upset to discover it missing, of course, and sorry that she could not pay Nora back, for she had been brought up to believe that one should pay one's debts promptly. But she would be seeing her parents at half-term, which was only a few days away, and they would see that she was in funds again. There were far more important things in life than money, anyway, thought Millicent, feverishly scribbling down notes. Such as music. Now, if something happened to stop her working at that, it really *would* be a disaster.

Half-term

The whole school was thrilled that it was half-term, though of course the more dignified fifth and sixth formers did not show their excitement in the riotous way that the younger girls did.

Coming out of the dining-room after breakfast on Saturday morning, Felicity and Susan were almost knocked over by a noisy group of first formers, all rushing to their common-room so that they could watch for their people to arrive.

'Slow down, you kids!' said Felicity sternly. 'It might be half-term, but that is no excuse to go tearing around the corridors like mad things.'

Miss Potts, walking by in time to overhear this, smiled to herself. She could remember having to reprimand young Felicity Rivers for exactly the same rowdy behaviour when she had been a first former, eagerly awaiting the arrival of her parents.

'Sorry, Felicity,' chorused the first formers. 'Sorry, Susan.'

As the younger girls walked away at a more measured pace, Susan said rather wistfully, 'What a thing it is to be a first former. I can remember when we were just like those kids, and felt so excited about half-term that we could hardly keep still.'

'Well, I feel just as excited now as I did when I was a first former,' admitted Felicity, with a grin. 'Of course, I have to keep it inside now that I'm a fifth former, but when I think about seeing Mother and Daddy again, and the marvellous time we have ahead of us, I could dance for joy!'

'What a pity that we are too old and sensible to do just that,' laughed Susan. 'I would love to see the faces of the younger girls if they saw us fifth formers dancing a jig all the way to the common-room.'

Mam'zelle, who happened to come round the corner at that moment, caught the tail end of this remark and gave a little start.

'Ah, *non*, Susan!' she said, with a frown. 'You must remember that you are a so-sensible fifth former now, and behave with dignity at all times. If the dear Miss Grayling were to come along and catch you dancing jigs around the school she would be most displeased.'

'Yes, Mam'zelle,' said Susan meekly, though her eyes twinkled.

'Don't worry, Mam'zelle,' said Felicity solemnly, taking Susan's arm. 'I shall escort Susan to the common-room, and make sure that she behaves as a fifth former should.'

Once the little French mistress was out of earshot, the two girls burst into laughter, and Susan said, 'Dear old Mam'zelle! Trust her to get the wrong end of the stick.'

The rest of the fifth formers were in the common-room waiting for their people to arrive, all except Delia, who had been called to Miss Grayling's room.

'I say,' said Amy to Bonnie. 'You don't think that Miss Grayling has found out about Delia taking Millicent's purse, do you?'

'For heaven's sake, keep your voice down, Amy!' hissed Bonnie, looking quickly over her shoulder to make sure that no one was close enough to overhear. 'How can Miss Grayling possibly know that, for we aren't even certain of it ourselves yet. And I don't think that Millicent reported the loss to Matron, so I doubt very much that Miss Grayling even knows that it's missing.'

But Delia certainly looked very down in the dumps about something when she returned to the common-room, and Gillian went across to her, saying kindly, 'What's up, old girl? Don't tell me that Miss Grayling gave you a row?'

'No, nothing like that,' said Delia rather dolefully. 'But she did give me some disappointing news. You see, my father is still overseas, so he won't be able to come and see me for half-term. Miss Grayling had a telegram from him a short while ago.'

The fifth formers were very sorry to hear this, even Amy, Lucy and Julie, who were all more than half-convinced that Delia was a thief.

'What a shame!' said Pam. 'But perhaps your aunt and cousins will come instead.'

'I doubt it,' said Delia, with a brave attempt at a smile. 'To be quite honest, I hope that they don't, for I don't like them and they don't like me. I would rather spend half-term on my own than in their company.'

'Well, you shan't spend it on your own,' said Gillian firmly. 'You are going to come out with me and my people.'

Delia's grey eyes lit up at this, and she cried, 'Oh, Gillian, that *is* decent of you! Are you sure that your parents won't mind me tagging along?'

'Of course not,' said Gillian. 'They will be pleased to know that I have made a friend.'

A warm glow came over Delia at this. Gillian had said that she was her friend! And that made the girl more convinced than ever that Gillian couldn't have taken Millicent's purse, for if she had, then she, Delia, must be a pretty poor judge of character.

'There are some parents arriving,' said June, who was standing by the window with Freddie. 'I say, they're mine! Most unlike them to get here so early. Come on, Freddie!'

Freddie, whose own parents were unable to come, was looking forward to a lively day out with June, her parents and one of her brothers.

As the two girls went out of the common-room, Pam and Nora moved across to take their places at the window.

'There are several cars arriving now,' said Nora. 'Can't say that I recognise any of the parents. Half a minute, though! Amy, that's your mother. I didn't recognise her at first, for she has a simply enormous hat on, but then she looked up and I knew who she was at once.'

There was no mistaking Amy's mother, for she was very beautiful indeed and always wore the most exquisite clothes.

Cars arrived thick and fast after that. Julie's people turned up next, then Nora's, and then Millicent's.

The girls noticed that Millicent looked very like her mother, for Mrs Moon had the same dark eyes, long face and intense expression. Her father, however, looked rather jolly, and Pam remarked under her breath, 'I can't imagine what he has to look jolly about, though, living with Millicent and her mother. I don't suppose that it's much fun!'

But Millicent looked very pleased to see her parents, her serious face breaking into a wide smile that quite transformed it.

Soon all of the parents had arrived, and Felicity was thrilled to be with her mother and father once more.

'Well, darling,' said Mr Rivers, giving Felicity a hug, then stepping back to take a good look at her. 'Being a fifth former obviously suits you, for you look very well indeed.'

'Yes, and I do believe that you've grown a little taller since the holidays,' said Mrs Rivers, slipping her arm through Felicity's.

'I don't know about that,' laughed Felicity. 'Though I probably look a little older, what with all the responsibility of being a wise, sensible fifth former!'

Delia, too, was enjoying herself, for, although she missed her father, Gillian's parents had gone out of their way to make her feel welcome.

'I do like your mother and father so much,' said Delia to Gillian, as the two of them went off to get cups of tea for Mr and Mrs Weaver – and themselves, of course. 'Your mother is so pretty and kind. And your father reminds me very much of my own, for he has exactly the same sense of humour.'

Gillian, of course, was delighted at this praise of her parents. The girl seemed much more like her old, carefree self today, for she was looking forward to spending a happy time with her people and her friend. What was more, there would be no time for her to practise either tennis or music today, or even to think about them, and Gillian had to admit that the break was very welcome.

The morning seemed to pass in a flash, for there were mistresses to talk to, and displays of needlework and art to look at. Then, of course, the girls had to show the parents their common-room and dormitory, not to mention the grounds, which always looked very beautiful at this time of year.

Once the parents had seen and admired everything, it was time to go out for lunch. Some parents, like Amy's and Bonnie's, took their daughters out to hotels or restaurants. Others, like Julie's and Felicity's, had brought magnificent picnics with them, which they took to the beach.

Mr and Mrs Weaver took Gillian and Delia to a very nice restaurant, where they had a most delicious lunch. Over pudding, while Gillian chatted to her father, Mrs

Weaver spoke to Delia, her warm, charming manner making it easy for the girl to relax. Soon Delia was confiding far more than she had intended to Mrs Weaver. Gillian's mother listened sympathetically, and laid her hand over Delia's, saying, 'Poor child! It must be terribly difficult living where you know you are not really wanted.'

'Well, I feel much happier now that I am at Malory Towers,' said Delia. 'It means that I only have to spend the holidays with my aunt and my cousins.'

Mrs Weaver looked thoughtful for a moment, then, at last, she said, 'You must come and stay with us for part of the holidays. Not if your father is home, of course, for I know that you will want to spend time with him. But if he is still at sea, then you will be most welcome, and I know that Gillian would like to have you.'

For a moment Delia was quite speechless, but at last she managed to stammer out her thanks.

Mrs Weaver smiled, and said, 'Well, my dear, there is a little something that you can do for me in return.'

'Of course,' said Delia at once, feeling quite prepared to do anything for this kind and sympathetic woman.

Mrs Weaver glanced up and, seeing that Gillian and her father were still deep in conversation, she lowered her voice, and said, 'I would like you to keep an eye on Gillian for me. She has told me all about the tennis team and the school orchestra, and I feel that she is over-working. She seems happy enough at the moment, but I know my daughter, and she has lost some of her sparkle.'

Delia nodded gravely, and said, 'Many of us fifth formers feel the same, Mrs Weaver. But Gillian simply can't be persuaded to give up one or the other. I shall do my best to try and make sure that she doesn't overdo things, though, you may be sure.'

In fact, Delia felt most honoured that Mrs Weaver had entrusted her with the task of looking after Gillian, and she meant to do her utmost to keep her word.

But there was no need to keep an eye on the girl at half-term, for Gillian seemed determined to push everything to the back of her mind and have fun. All of the fifth formers enjoyed their half-term break enormously, feeling tired but happy when it came to an end on Sunday evening.

'My word, what a super weekend,' said Pam with a contented sigh, as she settled down in an armchair.

'Wasn't it just?' agreed Freddie. 'June, your brother is an absolute scream!'

'Back to the grindstone tomorrow,' groaned Nora. 'Why does half-term always fly by so quickly?'

'You need cheering up, Nora,' said Susan, getting to her feet. 'And I know just the thing! My parents brought me a box of chocolates yesterday, from my grandmother, and I think that now is the time to open them.'

Susan went across to the big cupboard in the corner of the room and pulled open the door. Then she gave a little cry.

'What's up?' asked Felicity, alarmed.

'My chocolates!' said Susan. 'They're gone!'

Pam and Felicity went over to join her, Pam saying, 'They must be there! Chocolates don't just vanish into thin air.'

'Well, I put them on that shelf, and you can see for yourself that they are not there now, Pam,' said Susan, looking rather upset.

'I'll bet someone has moved them,' said Felicity, rummaging around in the cupboard. 'I was looking for a book in here the other day, and someone had knocked it on to the floor.'

But though she hunted high and low, the chocolates were nowhere to be found, and Pam said, 'Perhaps someone has hidden them for a joke.'

'Not a very funny one,' said Freddie. 'I was looking forward to one of those chocolates.'

'I can't think that anyone would have done that,' said June. 'Rather a first-form-ish sort of prank to play, if you ask me.'

'Yes, it is, rather,' said Julie. She glanced swiftly round the common-room, saw that Delia and Gillian were absent, and added, 'I don't think that Susan's chocolates have been hidden. I think that they have been stolen!'

The fifth formers looked rather shocked at this, and Pam said gravely, 'That's a very serious accusation, Julie. Do you have any reason for saying this?'

'Well, Millicent's purse went missing not so long ago,' said Julie. 'And it was never found.'

'I think that we should tell Pam what we know,' put

in Amy. 'After all, we said that we were going to once half-term was over anyway.'

Pam looked at Amy in surprise, and said, 'What are you talking about, Amy? Do you know something about the things that have gone missing?'

Quickly, Julie and Lucy told the others of how they had found Delia searching in Millicent's bag.

'And Bonnie and I caught her looking in Millicent's desk,' said Amy. 'Shortly before the purse disappeared.'

'It didn't disappear, it was stolen!' said June, scornfully. 'Just as Susan's chocolates have been. And it looks as if dear Delia is the thief.'

'You really should have told me all of this before, girls,' said Pam, looking very upset indeed, for she hated to think that there was a thief in the fifth form.

The others felt the same, and were disappointed in Delia, for most of them had grown to like her.

'I know that we should,' said Lucy. 'But we didn't want to put a damper on half-term, so thought that we would wait until the fun was over.'

'Well, it's certainly over now,' said Nora glumly. 'This has really brought us all down to earth with a bump.'

'What are you going to do, Pam?' asked June. 'Tackle Delia?'

'Not just yet,' said Pam, who had been looking thoughtful. 'I may have to, eventually, of course, but for now I think that we should all just watch her.'

'What's the good of that?' scoffed June. 'If Delia feels that she is being watched, she won't attempt to steal anything and we shall never catch her out.'

'Well, we will have to make sure that she doesn't know we are watching her,' said Pam firmly. 'We must all do our best to act normally when she is around, and be friendly to her. That way she won't suspect that we are on to her, and may slip up.'

'I don't agree,' said June stubbornly. 'If we speak to Delia now, she may own up and tell us where she has hidden the things she has stolen. I daresay that she has spent poor Millicent's money by now, but she can't possibly have eaten all of Susan's chocolates.'

'Well, it seems that we have a difference of opinion,' said Pam. 'So the only way to settle things is to vote. Would all those of you who are in favour of tackling Delia please raise your hands?'

Amy's hand shot up at once. Millicent, Julie, June and Lucy also raised theirs.

'That makes five of you,' said Pam. 'And who thinks that it would be better just to watch and wait?'

Of course, Pam herself put her hand up. So did Susan and Felicity, Nora and Bonnie. Freddie hesitated. June was her friend, and June wanted to get the whole thing out in the open. But Freddie couldn't quite believe that the pleasant-natured Delia was a thief. Once Freddie would have followed June's lead, but she had grown up quite a bit since those days, and now she decided that she must be true to herself and what she believed. If June took offence, then perhaps their friendship wasn't as strong as Freddie thought. So she put her hand up as well, and Pam said, 'Six. That means that we do as I suggest.'

'Gillian isn't here,' Amy pointed out. 'She hasn't had the chance to vote.'

'As Gillian is friendly with Delia, I think it's safe to assume that she would have voted with us,' said Felicity.

'Yes, and perhaps it would be best to keep Gillian in the dark,' said Susan. 'We don't want her warning Delia that she is under suspicion.'

'Quite right,' said Pam. 'June, I trust that you will abide by what has been decided?'

'Of course,' said June, looking surprised. 'Though I don't agree with it.'

'I realise that,' said Pam. 'The trouble is, June, that when you feel strongly about something, you rather have a tendency to go your own way when it comes to dealing with it.'

June flushed, for there had been several occasions in lower forms when she had confronted fellow pupils and accused them of something – sometimes wrongly. But June was older, and a little wiser, now, and didn't like being reminded of her conduct then.

'I can assure you that I have learned my lesson, Pam,' she said a little stiffly.

Pam was glad to hear it.

Just then, Delia and Gillian came in, both of them laughing and chattering happily.

Looking at the two of them, Felicity thought how much happier both of them seemed, now that they had become friends. Delia, in particular, had a sparkle in her eyes and a rosy glow to her open, honest face. For that was exactly what it was, thought Felicity, watching the girl closely, and feeling ever more certain that she couldn't be the thief.

But someone in the fifth form certainly was. And if it wasn't Delia, just who could it be?

Who is the thief?

The fifth formers stuck to their word and watched Delia carefully. When she volunteered to stay behind and tidy up the class-room for Miss James, Felicity and Susan hid themselves behind a pillar outside the class-room, and watched.

Delia was most conscientious, humming softly to herself as she wiped the blackboard, then she carefully put away the pile of books on Miss James's desk. The girl picked up a crumpled ball of paper that had fallen on the floor and dropped it in the wastepaper bin, then she went round the room making sure that all the chairs were neatly pushed under the desks. But at no time did she open any of the desks, or do anything remotely suspicious.

When her work was done, she moved towards the door, and Felicity and Susan slipped quietly away.

'Well,' said Felicity, as the two of them walked down the corridor. 'If Delia really *is* the thief, that would have been the perfect opportunity for her to go hunting in all of our desks, looking for things to steal.'

'Yet she didn't take it,' said Susan thoughtfully. 'I always found it hard to believe that old Delia was a thief, and now I find it even harder. I suppose we had better go and report to Pam.'

Pam was sitting on the grass in the sunshine, along with Nora, June and Freddie, and she looked up as Felicity and Susan approached.

'Well?' she said. 'Anything to report?'

'Not a thing,' said Felicity, sitting down next to the girl. 'Delia simply tidied up, but she didn't go in any of the desks.'

'I spied on her when she was alone in the common-room the other day,' said Freddie. 'And she didn't try to take anything then, either. The only time that she went to the cupboard was to put her knitting away.'

'Another ideal opportunity wasted,' said Susan. 'I really do think that Delia is innocent, and that we are on the wrong track.'

'Well, I don't,' said June, in her forthright way. 'I believe that she knows we are on to her, and that is why she is behaving herself at the moment. As soon as we drop our guard and stop watching her all the time, things will start to disappear again. Mark my words!'

With that, June got to her feet and said, 'Well, I'm off to tennis practice. Anyone coming?'

Freddie got up, and Felicity said, 'Susan and I will be there in a few minutes. I just want to sit and enjoy the sunshine for a little while.'

The four girls sat in comfortable, companionable silence for a few moments, enjoying the feel of the warm sun on their faces, then Susan suddenly said, 'You know, in a way I'm sorry that we didn't catch Delia trying to steal something.'

'Whatever do you mean?' asked Nora, startled. 'I thought that you liked Delia.'

'I do,' answered Susan. 'But now that it is looking as though Delia may not be the thief, it means that everyone else in the fifth form is under suspicion.'

'Exactly what I was thinking,' said Pam, sounding very troubled. 'Not a pleasant thought, is it?'

'Gosh!' exclaimed Nora, looking dismayed. 'I hadn't thought of that. How horrible!'

'It is horrible,' said Felicity. 'And it makes it even more important for us to clear this up and catch the thief as soon as possible.'

'Well, if any of you have any ideas of how we could do that, I'd be jolly glad if you would share them with me,' sighed Pam. 'For I'm stumped!'

But the others couldn't think of anything either, and at last Susan jumped up, saying, 'Come on, Felicity. Let's go and get some tennis practice in. Perhaps a little exercise will get our brains moving!'

Gillian was also at the tennis-courts, for now that half-term was over, she was working just as hard as before.

It seemed that the break had done her good, for the dark shadows beneath her eyes had lightened, and she was playing against her opponent, a West Tower girl, with renewed energy and determination.

'Good show, Gillian!' yelled June from the sidelines, as the girl sent a ball whizzing past the other girl. Then she turned to Felicity and Susan, saying, 'Ah, good, you're here. How would you like a game of doubles against Freddie and me?'

The two girls agreed to this eagerly, and took their places on the court. Felicity and Susan had played together so often that they knew one another's game very well indeed, and it stood them in good stead, for they beat their opponents comfortably.

Felicity, knowing how June hated to be beaten at anything, felt a little apprehensive as the four of them walked to the net to shake hands. But, to her surprise, June was grinning broadly.

Seeing the look of astonishment on Felicity's face, June laughed, and said, 'Are you wondering why I'm so pleased, Felicity? Well, it's because this proves that I have chosen exactly the right pair to represent us in the doubles against Summerfield Hall. I couldn't be more pleased to be beaten, for I know that you and Susan will do us proud in the tournament.'

Felicity and Susan felt pleased as well. Why, June really *was* learning the meaning of team spirit!

'Gillian is going to do well, too,' said June, looking across at the girl, who had finished her game and was sitting on the grass. 'I admit that I was a little worried about her, but now she's back on form and fighting fit.'

Gillian certainly felt fighting fit, and thought that it was marvellous what a couple of days' relaxation could do.

And it was just as well that she felt rested and

refreshed, for there was another orchestra rehearsal the following day. With that in mind, Gillian took herself off to one of the music-rooms to practise. But Delia, with Mrs Weaver's words in mind, went after her, calling, 'Where are you going, Gillian?'

'To play my violin,' answered Gillian. 'Come with me if you want. You can listen, and tell me what you think.'

Delia agreed at once, for she loved music. And she could keep an eye on Gillian, too, and make sure that she wasn't overdoing it.

There was a rapt expression on Delia's face as she perched on a stool and listened to Gillian play. Soon the girl was swaying from side to side again as she lost herself in the music, almost falling off her stool at one point!

Then Gillian began her solo, and, unable to stop herself, Delia began softly singing the words that she had written to accompany the tune. Now it was Gillian's turn to listen, and, as she did, her fingers gradually stopped moving, until the only sound that filled the room was that of Delia's sweet voice.

At first Delia didn't realise that Gillian had stopped playing, and continued to sing. Then she became aware that she was no longer being accompanied, and her voice died away.

'Sorry,' she said gruffly, looking rather self-conscious. 'I just got carried away. Don't know what came over me!'

'Heavens, don't apologise!' cried Gillian. 'Why, it sounded marvellous. I had no idea that Millicent wrote words as well.'

115

Delia hesitated, then decided that she didn't want to mislead Gillian, who had been a true friend to her.

So, rather reluctantly, she confessed, 'Actually, Millicent didn't write the words. I did.'

Gillian gave a gasp, and exclaimed, 'You dark horse, Delia! You've been telling us that you're such a duffer, and all the time you have been hiding this wonderful talent for song-writing.'

'I would hardly call it a talent,' said Delia, turning red at this unaccustomed praise. 'It was just a little rhyme that I jotted down at the first rehearsal.'

'Nonsense!' said Gillian. 'The words are simply beautiful, and they fit the music perfectly. And you have such a lovely singing voice.'

'Do I?' said Delia, looking most astonished.

'Yes,' said Gillian firmly. 'So sweet and pure. I know! Why don't we go down to the common-room and you can sing for the others? They will be absolutely amazed! I'll bring my violin and accompany you.'

But poor Delia was far too nervous and lacking in confidence to even think of such a thing. And she was more than half inclined to believe that Gillian was only praising her so extravagantly because she was her friend. Why, she often used to sing at her aunt's house, as she helped with the daily chores, and the reaction she got from her aunt and cousins was quite different.

Her mean-spirited cousins had told her that she sounded like a parrot squawking, while her aunt had sternly ordered her to be quiet, as the racket Delia was making was giving her a headache.

The fifth formers probably wouldn't be so unkind, for they were well brought-up, polite girls. But how dreadful it would be if they laughed at her behind her back.

'I really couldn't!' said Delia, shaking her head and looking terrified. 'My voice isn't good enough, and I would feel so nervous that it would shake terribly.'

Gillian disagreed wholeheartedly with this, but realised that if she tried to push Delia into performing for the others it would simply make her more scared. Lack of confidence was at the root of the girl's problem, she realised, and Gillian's mouth pursed as she thought that Delia's strict aunt and beastly cousins were responsible.

As Delia's friend, she really ought to do something about building the girl's confidence, but she had taken on so much herself that it would be difficult to find the time. Suddenly a thought occurred to her, and she said, 'Delia, I shan't try and persuade you to sing for the others, but if you would sing along with me sometimes when I rehearse, I really think that it would help me.'

'Really?' said Delia, surprised and pleased.

'Really,' said Gillian, solemnly. 'And who knows, perhaps you can think of some more words that you can set to the music. That would be super!'

'All right then, I shall,' agreed Delia, thinking that this was something that she would enjoy doing, and that she would feel quite comfortable singing for Gillian, and even letting her see any words she composed, for she knew that her friend would not make fun of her.

So Delia sung until she was hoarse, and when she couldn't sing any more, she sat and listened to her friend playing.

Gillian played the same few bars over and over again, for there was one note that she simply *couldn't* get right, no matter what. By the end of it, she had managed to get the note right, but she was looking pale and strained again.

Delia noticed this, and could have kicked herself. She had promised Mrs Weaver that she would look after Gillian, and make sure that she didn't tire herself out. And she had been so carried away with her singing that she had failed, and let Mrs Weaver down.

Heavens, they must have been up here in the music-room for simply ages!

In fact it was almost ten o'clock, and the others were all getting ready for bed when Delia and Gillian went to the dormitory.

'Where have you two been?' asked Felicity.

'In one of the music-rooms,' answered Gillian, with a yawn. 'Delia has been listening to me practise my violin.'

Millicent looked at the girl with approval, saying, 'That's what I like to see! A bit of dedication and hard work.'

June was less pleased, for she didn't like to see any member of the tennis team working hard for anyone other than herself. But June saw how tired and pale Gillian looked, and held her tongue.

At last everyone settled down, and Pam turned the lights out. There was no need, of course, for her to remind everyone of the no-talking rule, for as fifth formers the girls would not have dreamed of disobeying it.

One by one, the girls dropped off to sleep. Gillian was first, for she was completely exhausted. And Delia was last, for she had a lot to think about. Her feelings were mixed, for, on the one hand, she felt ridiculously pleased at the way Gillian had complimented her on her singing and the words that she had written to Millicent's tune. On the other, she couldn't help feeling that she hadn't done a very good job at getting her friend to spend more time relaxing, and less on tennis and music.

Well, tomorrow was a new day, and Delia vowed that she would work in earnest towards keeping the promise she had made to Mrs Weaver.

The thief strikes again

There was a shock in store for Amy the following morning. The girl's mother had given her a very expensive bottle of French perfume at half-term, which she had displayed proudly on her bedside cabinet. All of the fifth formers had been allowed to sniff at it, but no one had been allowed so much as a dab of the scent, for, as Amy had said, in her haughty way, 'Mummy went to a great deal of trouble to get it for me. It's very expensive, you know, and quite difficult to get hold of.'

'I should put the stopper back in, at once, Amy,' June had said gravely. 'Otherwise the scent will escape and all you will be left with is a bottle of liquid with no smell at all.'

'Rubbish!' Amy had said, though she had looked a little doubtful.

'It's perfectly true,' Freddie had said, with a completely straight face. 'My aunt once had a bottle of perfume, and she forgot to put the stopper back in, and the following day the smell had all gone! My aunt was frightfully upset, of course, for it was a birthday present from my uncle, and she had to throw it away.'

Amy was never *quite* sure when June and Freddie

were pulling her leg, but, to be on the safe side, she had put the stopper back in the scent bottle at once, and placed it carefully on her cabinet.

The others had known that June and Freddie were having a joke, and had smiled to themselves, even Bonnie unable to hide a grin at her friend's confused expression.

This morning, Amy, who always took a great deal of care over her appearance, was sitting on the edge of the bed, brushing her silky blonde hair, when her eye fell upon the cabinet, and she gave a little shriek.

There were several fifth formers in the dormitory, and they jumped, Pam saying, 'For goodness' sake, Amy, *must* you squeal like that? Whatever is the matter?'

'My perfume!' cried Amy, looking very distressed. 'It's gone!'

Everyone gathered round at once, Bonnie saying, 'Are you sure that it hasn't fallen on the floor, Amy?'

The fifth formers began to hunt for the missing perfume bottle, looking under beds and behind cabinets. But there was no sign of it.

'Where *can* it have gone!' asked Amy, who really was very upset, for expensive possessions meant a great deal to the girl.

'I should think that it has gone to the same place as Millicent's purse and Susan's chocolates,' said June, in a hard little voice. 'The thief has struck again!'

'Then we must tackle her,' said Amy. 'It's one thing to take a box of chocolates, or a purse with only a few pounds in it, but that perfume is most exclusive, and –'

'Oh, do be quiet, Amy,' said Felicity, exasperated. 'It isn't the value of the things that have been stolen that is important. It is the fact that we have a thief among us.'

'Quite right,' said Pam, well aware that, as head-girl, it was up to her to take some action. But she couldn't think quite what to do, for it really was a very tricky situation.

June, though, had very definite ideas, and she said, 'Delia must be hiding the things somewhere. Perhaps they are in her cabinet. I vote we take a look.'

But Pam said firmly, 'No. I refuse to do something so sly and underhand. Besides, we have all been watching Delia, and she hasn't taken anything, although she has had several chances.'

'Well, someone has the stolen things,' said Amy. 'And there's no denying that a bedside cabinet would make a jolly good hiding place.'

'Very well,' said Pam. 'After breakfast we shall all come to the dormitory, and I shall ask everyone to open their bedside cabinets, so that we can see what is in there. Does everyone agree that that is fair?'

The others nodded solemnly, and went to join the rest of the fifth form for breakfast. Slipping into her seat, Felicity stole a glance at Delia, sitting across the table next to Gillian.

The girl was tucking into toast and marmalade, looking relaxed and happy as she chattered to her friend, and Felicity thought that surely Delia could not look like that if she was hiding a guilty secret.

At last the meal was over, and Julie and Lucy got to their feet.

'We're off for a ride,' said Lucy. 'It's a beautiful day, and we don't want to miss a second of it.'

'Hold on a minute, please,' said Pam. 'I would like you all to come up to the dormitory for a few moments.'

Those girls who hadn't been present when it was discovered that Amy's perfume was missing exchanged puzzled glances, and Julie said, 'Why, Pam?'

'I shall tell you when we get there,' replied Pam. 'It won't take long, and I would be very grateful if you all do as I ask.'

So the fifth formers trooped back upstairs, and, once they were in the dormitory, Pam said, 'Can you all stand by your cabinets, please.'

The girls did as they were asked, Pam standing by hers as well. Then she said, 'I would like you all to open the doors so that we can see what is inside.'

'Why?' asked Gillian, looking rather bewildered.

'Well, Gillian,' said Pam. 'I hate to say this, but it appears that we have a thief in the fifth form. As you know, Millicent's purse disappeared a while ago, then Susan's chocolates, and now Amy's perfume has gone. It's possible that the thief has hidden the things in her cabinet, so we are going to check all of them. Does anyone object?'

No one did, and June, looking hard at Delia, was forced to admit to herself that if the girl was putting on an act, it was a jolly good one. She looked very shocked indeed, but not at all guilty, and was among the first to pull open her cabinet door. There was nothing in there, of course, but her own belongings, and as Pam went along looking inside all the cabinets, it soon became apparent that no one was hiding anything.

At last she said, 'Felicity, will you look in my cabinet, please, then I can put myself in the clear as well.'

Felicity did as she was asked, peering into Pam's cabinet, and moving a few things so that she could get a good look.

'Not a thing,' she said, when she had finished her search. 'Not that I expected Pam, of all people, to be hiding stolen goods.'

The girls all felt secretly rather relieved that nothing had been found in the dormitory, yet uneasy that the thief was still at large.

'A bit of a waste of time, really,' said June to Freddie afterwards. 'The thief has obviously found a safer hiding place, and we are no closer to unmasking her.'

Amy, of course, was most displeased, and she stalked up to Pam, saying crossly, 'I think that we ought to report the matter to Miss Grayling. Whoever took my perfume simply can't be allowed to get away with it. The Head must call the police, and –'

'My dear Amy, I am quite sure that the police have more important matters to deal with than your missing perfume,' said Pam coolly. 'Besides, if the police are called it will mean bad publicity for the school, and the Head won't want that if it can be avoided.'

'Then what is to be done?' demanded Amy.

'I don't know,' admitted Pam, with a sigh.

'I have an idea,' said Bonnie, coming forward.

'Then by all means let's hear it,' said Pam.

Bonnie glanced round, to make sure that no one else was in the room but the three of them. The others had all gone, and as Bonnie felt quite certain that neither Pam nor Amy was the thief, she was able to speak freely.

But first, Bonnie took something from her cabinet, and held it out to show the other two. It was a large brooch, sparkly, shiny and glittery, and Amy wrinkled her long nose in distaste, saying, 'What an awful thing! Really, Bonnie, I always thought that you had good taste.'

Bonnie laughed, and said, 'Quite hideous, isn't it? My aunt gave it to me for my birthday, and I would be most grateful if someone would steal it, for I couldn't possibly wear it.'

'What are you suggesting, Bonnie?' asked Pam, with a frown.

'Well,' said Bonnie, her eyes dancing impishly. 'If I was to leave this lying around somewhere, surely the thief won't be able to resist it. It's not particularly valuable, but it *looks* as if it might be.'

'Yes, but I don't see what good it would do,' said Pam. 'Our thief would be certain to take the brooch, but it won't help us to find out who she is.'

'Ah, but it will,' said Bonnie. 'Look!'

She held out her hand, and Pam and Amy saw that her fingers were covered with glitter.

'It comes off, see?' said Bonnie. 'And although it seems to rub off the brooch quite easily, it tends to stick to the fingers unless you wash your hands thoroughly.'

'So once the brooch has been taken, all we have to do is look at everyone's hands!' said Amy excitedly. 'My word, Bonnie, what a super idea!'

'It *is* a good idea!' said Pam, looking pleased. 'But are you sure you don't mind risking your brooch, Bonnie?'

'Not at all,' said Bonnie, with a smile. 'The thief is quite welcome to it. I shall put it on top of my bedside cabinet, where she can't help but notice it.'

'Yes, it does rather draw one's attention,' said Amy, with a shudder. 'It sparkles so much that I daresay we shall still be able to see it when the lights are out!'

Bonnie went to wash the glitter from her hands, then she and Amy went off to the common-room together, while Pam sought out Nora and bore her off for a walk along the cliffs.

As it was Sunday morning, the girls were busily engaged in their own activities. Julie and Lucy, of course, were out riding, Millicent was poring over her music, and June, helped by Freddie, was making out a list of practice times for the lower school.

Felicity and Susan were helping in the school garden, and even Gillian was enjoying a little fresh air, for Delia, mindful of her promise to the girl's mother, had insisted that she come outside for a stroll around the gardens.

Gillian had been reluctant at first, saying fretfully,

'I really should be practising my music, for there is a rehearsal this afternoon.'

'You spent most of yesterday evening practising,' Delia had pointed out, her tone of voice unusually firm. 'I think it would do you much more good to spend a little time outdoors, then you will turn up for rehearsal refreshed, and with a clear head.'

Gillian had been forced to admit that there was something in that, and said, 'It does seem a shame to be cooped up indoors on such a beautiful day. Very well, Delia, I'll come with you.'

And the two girls had whiled away a pleasant couple of hours idly strolling about the grounds, passing the time of day with Mam'zelle Dupont, admiring the beautiful blooms in the Head's garden, and simply sitting on the grass chatting about this and that.

'Well, what a nice, peaceful morning it has been!' said Gillian happily, as she and Delia made their way to the dining-room for lunch. 'I would never have guessed that simply doing nothing could be such fun.'

Delia laughed, and said, 'I do wish that I could come and watch the rehearsal this afternoon. I shall be quite at a loose end.'

'Well, come along then,' said Gillian. 'Perhaps it will help me to play better if I can see a friendly face.'

'I can't,' said Delia, with a grimace. 'You know that Millicent has banned anyone who isn't actually in the orchestra from attending rehearsals.'

'Yes, but I think that she only said that because some of

the younger girls who came to watch were fooling about, and distracting the orchestra,' said Gillian. 'She knows that no fifth former would behave like that, so I am quite sure she won't object if you want to sit and watch.'

Millicent didn't object, for she didn't want to upset Gillian, and had noticed how friendly she and Delia had become. So she smiled brightly, and said, 'Of course, Delia is most welcome to sit and watch. I know that she can be trusted not to distract anyone.'

But there were discontented mutterings from some of the orchestra members as Delia took a seat at the front of the hall.

'My friend Meg would have liked to come and watch us rehearse,' said Kathy, of the third form. 'But Millicent simply wouldn't hear of it.'

'I should have liked to bring one or two of the East Tower girls along for support, too,' said Anne, scowling. 'Millicent said no to that as well. It just isn't fair! There is one rule for Gillian, and another for the rest of us.'

'Yet Millicent expects us to play our hearts out for her,' said Janet. 'Well, I think it's about time she gave something back.'

'Yes, it really is difficult to do something whole-heartedly when we are being treated so unfairly,' said Jessie. 'I, for one, am beginning to wish that I had never put my name down to join this beastly orchestra.'

'Quiet, please, everyone!' said Millicent sharply. 'Let's begin the rehearsal. I would like you to play the whole piece through, from beginning to end.'

'What if someone makes a mistake?' called out Janet.

'If you have been practising as you should, there shouldn't be any mistakes,' said Millicent briskly. 'However, if anyone *does* play a wrong note, I want her to ignore it and carry on. What I am trying to do today is to get an idea of how the whole thing will sound.'

So the orchestra played 'Summer Serenade' all the way through, and it sounded so beautiful that even Millicent was pleased, and managed a few words of praise.

'I can hear that you *have* been practising hard,' she said, with a smile. 'Well done.'

Then she glanced at her watch, and said, 'As you have done so well, I think that you deserve a short break. We will start again in fifteen minutes.'

With that, Millicent swept from the room. Some of the orchestra followed her, keen to get a breath of fresh air, while others sat on the chairs in the hall, simply glad of a rest.

'Well, wonders will never cease!' said Jessie. 'Fancy Millicent allowing us a break!'

'And she praised us,' said Anne. '*All* of us, not just Gillian. Well, if Millicent keeps this up, I daresay it won't be so bad being in the orchestra, after all.'

But Anne had spoken too soon, for the rehearsal, which had started so promisingly, was to end in disaster.

A few minutes before the orchestra were due to take their places again, Kathy's friend Meg, along with several of her fellow third formers, peeped into the hall. Seeing that Millicent was not present, they ventured in, and the rather cheeky Meg asked, 'Where's the slave-driver?'

Kathy giggled, and answered, 'She's given us a well-earned break and gone off for a walk.'

'Yes, and I think it might be a good idea if you kids disappear before she comes back,' said Gillian. 'Unless you want one of Millicent's scolds.'

'Pooh!' scoffed Meg, forgetting for a moment that she was talking to a fifth former. 'I see that *your* friend is allowed to watch the rehearsal, Gillian.'

Gillian's eyes flashed angrily, and she said, 'How dare you speak to me like that? Apologise at once!'

Meg scowled, and hesitated for a moment, then, as she saw Gillian reach into her pocket for the punishment book that all the fifth and sixth formers carried with them, she blurted out, 'I'm sorry. I didn't mean to sound rude.'

All would have been well, and the third formers would have left quietly, but just then Millicent returned, and, on spotting the youngsters, went 'up in the air', as Kathy put it.

'Kathy, didn't I tell you that no one was allowed to watch the rehearsal without my permission?' she snapped. 'I don't take kindly to being disobeyed. You kids, clear off at once!'

Now Meg, who had just been thinking herself lucky to have escaped a punishment for cheeking Gillian, felt nettled. Why did Millicent have to be so autocratic and unpleasant all the time?

She glanced round at the rest of the third formers, all

of whom were eyeing Millicent apprehensively, and waiting to take their lead from Meg. And Meg knew that she would go up in her form's estimation no end if she stood up to the bossy Millicent.

'Why should we leave?' she asked defiantly. 'I'm sure that we have as much right to be here as Delia.'

There were murmurs of agreement from the third formers, and Millicent said, 'Delia is a fifth former, and can be relied on to behave. Unlike you youngsters. Now push off, before I dish out punishments to the lot of you!'

'Just as we were hoping that Millicent had turned over a new leaf,' murmured Janet to Anne and Jessie. 'I thought it was too good to be true.'

But Meg, with the admiring eyes of her form upon her, wasn't giving up without a fight, and began to argue with Millicent.

Thoroughly exasperated, Millicent pulled out her punishment book, quickly wrote something on one of the pages, then ripped it out and handed it to the furious Meg.

'There!' she said. 'And let it be a lesson to you to show a little respect to your elders!'

Meg was shocked when she looked at the piece of paper and saw that she had been given a hundred lines, but it was worth it when she saw the admiration on the faces of her friends.

'Never mind, Meg,' whispered Kathy, who felt quite furious with Millicent. 'I'll do half of them for you.'

'Be quiet, Kathy, and get to your place, please,' said Millicent sharply. 'And once your friends have buzzed off, you can play your part again, for I noticed several wrong notes earlier. Perhaps if you spent more time practising, and less fooling around with your friends, you would be a better musician.'

Poor Kathy's face burned, for she knew that Millicent was deliberately trying to humiliate her in front of her form. She glanced round at her friends, saw their sympathetic glances, and something inside her snapped.

'Very well,' she said coldly. 'If I am such a poor musician, Millicent, perhaps you had better find someone else to take my place.'

And, before the astonished eyes of the orchestra, Kathy picked up her trumpet and stalked towards the door. She was followed by her friends, all of them delighted that she had made a stand.

Millicent, however, was thoroughly dismayed, and called out, 'Kathy, wait! You can't just leave the orchestra like that! I shall report you to Miss Grayling.'

'You can't,' retorted Kathy in a tight little voice. 'I joined the orchestra of my own free will, and I am leaving of my own free will. Neither you, Millicent, nor Miss Grayling herself, can force me to continue.'

And Millicent was left quite speechless, for once, because she knew that Kathy was right. Blow, now what was she to do? The competition was only four weeks away, and now she, Millicent, had to find another trumpet player who could learn the music in such a short time. And Millicent had to admit that, in spite of her harsh words, she would never find another one as good as Kathy.

Mutiny in the orchestra

Millicent did find another trumpet player, but the girl was a first former who hadn't been playing for very long and wasn't up to Kathy's standard. And it seemed that Millicent had learned nothing from her mistakes, for at the next rehearsal she was so bad-tempered that Jessie also resigned from the orchestra, leaving another gap to be filled.

'These kids have no staying power,' Millicent complained to Anne, when the rehearsal was over. 'They simply can't stick at anything.'

Anne, who had been on the verge of walking out herself on more than one occasion, said nothing. Millicent was so thick-skinned that she simply couldn't see that if only she would treat her orchestra with a little more respect and kindness she would get better results.

Jessie had played the cello, and Millicent knew that there were only two other girls in the school who played that instrument – Lizzie, of the third form and Belinda of the fourth.

As Lizzie was the better player, Millicent approached her first. But, out of loyalty to her friend Kathy, Lizzie flatly refused to be part of the orchestra.

'No thanks,' she said shortly. 'I don't want to give up my free time only to be shouted at and humiliated, as poor Kathy was. And now you have driven Jessie away too. If you're not careful, Millicent, you won't have an orchestra left to conduct!'

Millicent smarted at Lizzie's words, but they sank in, and she made up her mind to be a little less hard on the players.

Belinda, who had heard about Jessie's resignation, and also knew that Millicent had asked Lizzie to replace her, wasn't at all pleased to be third choice. But, with Lizzie's words in mind, Millicent was unusually humble when she spoke to the girl, and soon Belinda found herself feeling sorry for the fifth former and agreed to take Jessie's place in the orchestra.

The fifth form knew of Millicent's troubles, of course, for word travelled fast, but few of them had much sympathy to spare for her. They thought that she only had herself to blame. Besides, they had other things to worry about, for the thief had struck again.

Poor Nora was most upset to discover that her watch, which had been a present from her parents, had gone missing. And Julie was very puzzled indeed when her purse disappeared.

'It was empty,' she told some of the others, as they sat on the lawn one sunny afternoon. 'Not so much as a penny in it, for I'm quite broke until my people send me some money next week.'

'Why on earth would someone steal an empty purse?' said Susan.

'Perhaps the thief didn't realise it was empty when she took it,' said Felicity.

'Well, that will have been one in the eye for her,' said Pam, with satisfaction. 'Gosh, wouldn't I have loved to see her face when she opened your purse, Julie, only to find nothing there!'

'Yes, but everyone in our form knew that you were broke, Julie,' said Lucy, who had been looking thoughtful. 'You were complaining about it in the common-room only the other night, remember?'

'That's right,' said June. 'And you were complaining jolly loudly, too, so we all heard you!'

'Not all of us,' said Freddie. 'Only those of us who were in the common-room that evening.'

'Let's think,' said Nora. 'It was Friday evening. Who was missing?'

'Delia and Gillian,' said Felicity. 'Gillian had gone to practise her violin, and Delia went with her.'

'Millicent was missing, too,' said June. 'I remember her saying that she had been so wrapped up in her composing and orchestra rehearsals that she was quite neglecting her practice, so she went off to one of the music-rooms as well.'

'I think we can rule out Millicent,' said Susan. 'She's hardly likely to take her own purse.'

'Unless she is trying to throw us off the scent,' said Bonnie.

'What do you mean?' asked Pam.

'Well, Millicent may have been pretending that she had her purse stolen,' answered Bonnie. 'So that we wouldn't suspect her of being the thief.'

'Well, in that case I could be the thief too,' said Amy. 'I wasn't in the common-room when Julie said that she had no money, for Matron had sent for me. So I could easily have pretended that my perfume had been stolen, then taken Julie's purse.'

But no one seriously suspected Amy. The girl had her faults, but she wasn't dishonest. Besides, Amy's parents were wealthy, and she always had as much money as she wanted, so there was no need for her to steal.

Yet the one thing that seemed to hold no attraction for the thief was Bonnie's sparkly brooch. It had lain untouched on her bedside cabinet for several days now, and, lowering her voice, Bonnie murmured to Amy, 'It's so ugly that no one even wants to steal the beastly thing!'

'Well, at least we know that our thief has good taste,' said Amy, with a laugh. 'She took my expensive perfume, yet won't touch your horrid little brooch!'

'Yes, it's a pity,' said Bonnie. 'For that would have trapped her nicely. If only we could find something a little more tasteful that we could catch her out with.'

Amy snapped her fingers suddenly. 'But we can!' she said. 'The thief has my perfume, Bonnie. And what is the use of stealing a bottle of perfume if one isn't going to wear it.'

'Of course!' said Bonnie, her eyes lighting up. 'Well

done, Amy. Perhaps all we have to do is follow our noses. We'll concentrate on Millicent, Delia and Gillian for now, as they are the three who were absent when Julie was talking about having no money.'

Millicent was extremely irritated that evening when Bonnie sat down next to her in the common-room that evening and began to sniff noisily. The girl was reading a book about great composers, and Bonnie was ruining her concentration. At last she flung she book aside, and said crossly, 'Bonnie, *must* you do that?'

'Sorry, Millicent,' said Bonnie, giving another loud sniff. 'I think I have a cold coming on.'

'Well, for heaven's sake use a handkerchief!' said Millicent. 'Or better still, go and sit somewhere else.'

Bonnie was finished with Millicent anyway, for all she had been able to smell was the faint scent of soap and talcum powder. Quite pleasant, but nothing like the strong, distinctive scent of Amy's perfume. She went across to join her friend, who had just been speaking to Delia and Gillian, and was now looking rather glum.

'Well, neither Delia nor Gillian are wearing my perfume,' Amy sighed. 'All I could smell on Gillian was shampoo, and Delia didn't seem to smell of anything at all. How about Millicent?'

'No, Millicent wasn't wearing your perfume either,' said Bonnie. 'Although, now that I come to think of it, the thief might think it was too risky to use the perfume at school. She might have decided to take it home and wear it during the hols.'

Amy didn't look at all pleased at this thought, but brightened when Bonnie said, 'Cheer up! There are still several weeks to go before we break up, which leaves plenty of time for the thief to slip up. So there is still a chance that you may get your perfume back untouched.'

But the thief didn't slip up over the next few days. Pam lost her best fountain pen, and June was simply furious when a tie-pin that she had bought for her father's birthday was taken. June always hated the thought of anyone getting one over on her, and she took the theft very hard indeed.

'I'll find out who it is, you see if I don't!' she vowed to Freddie. 'And when I do, my gosh I'll make her sorry.'

'Yes, but what on earth would a schoolgirl want with a tie-pin?' asked Freddie, puzzled. 'I mean to say, it can't be any use to her at all.'

'Perhaps the thief means to give it to *her* father as a present,' said June grimly.

'You know, June, I don't often agree with Amy, but perhaps she is right and we ought to report this to the Head,' said Freddie. 'It really is going too far now, with something vanishing almost every day.'

June heartily agreed that the thief was going too far, and getting much too sure of herself, but she still felt reluctant to report the matter to Miss Grayling. Much better, she thought, if the fifth form could have the satisfaction of catching the thief themselves, and then hauling her before the Head!

Something very surprising happened the following

day. The girls had just gone down to breakfast, but, as she reached the bottom of the stairs, Bonnie realised that she had forgotten her handkerchief, and, as she had the beginnings of a horrid summer cold, went back up to the dormitory to fetch it. And then what a shock she got! For the brooch that she had put out to catch the thief was gone!

The girl almost quivered with excitement, for she had quite given up hope of the thief falling into her trap. But now it seemed that she had. And it would be an easy matter, at the breakfast table, to take a look at everyone's hands and see whose was covered in the tell-tale glitter. Bonnie couldn't be certain whether the brooch had been there when she had woken up, for she had forgotten to look. It could have been taken overnight, or perhaps someone had sneaked it off the cabinet while the fifth formers were getting ready for breakfast. That would have been an easy matter, for there was always a lot of to-ing and fro-ing first thing in the morning, with girls in and out of the bathroom all the time.

Hastily, Bonnie stuffed her handkerchief into her pocket and made her way down to the dining-room, where she slipped into her seat, between Pam and Amy. Quickly, she whispered to both girls, telling them what had happened.

They were most astonished, and Pam said in a low voice, 'Well, it looks as if we are about to catch our thief.'

'But what if she has washed the glitter off her hands?' whispered Amy.

'It's awfully hard to get off,' said Bonnie. 'No matter how you scrub. When I handled it the other day I still had little specks stuck to my fingers the next day.'

'I say, Delia!' said Pam, raising her voice. 'Pass the marmalade, would you?'

Delia did so, and Pam took the opportunity to take a good look at her hands. They were spotless, and Pam turned to Bonnie and Amy, giving a quick shake of her head.

Over breakfast the three girls had an opportunity to inspect the hands of all of the fifth formers, even those that they were certain were quite innocent. But, by the time the meal was over, they were no further forward, for none of the fifth formers had so much as a speck of glitter on her hands.

'Well, I'm baffled!' said Pam, as she left the dining-room with Bonnie and Amy. 'Bonnie, are you absolutely certain that the brooch was in its usual place when you went to bed last night?'

'Absolutely,' said Bonnie with a firm little nod. 'But I can't be sure whether it disappeared overnight, or this morning.'

'So much for our trap!' said Amy disconsolately. 'What a let-down.'

'Not entirely,' said Bonnie with a smile. 'At least I have got rid of that dreadful brooch!'

Pam laughed at that, and said, 'Well, at least something good has come out of this awful business for you, Bonnie. But the thief is still running rings round us.

I'm afraid that, if we can't clear this matter up ourselves very soon, we really will have no choice but to report it to Miss Grayling.'

Bonnie's cold seemed to grow steadily worse during the first lesson, which was French. Mam'zelle Dupont noticed that the girl, who was one of her favourites, was sneezing rather a lot.

'Are you ill, *ma petite*?' she asked, kindly.

'Oh, it's just a little cold, Mam'zelle,' said Bonnie, smiling bravely. 'Nothing to worry about.'

Then she gave the most enormous sneeze, so loud that Freddie, sitting next to her, said afterwards that it almost blew her papers off the desk.

'*Tiens!*' cried Mam'zelle, quite alarmed. 'This is no little cold, *ma chère* Bonnie, this is a great big cold, for it makes you do a great big sneeze. You must go to Matron at once!'

Bonnie wasn't very thrilled at the thought of going to Matron, whose remedy for colds was a large dose of extremely nasty-tasting medicine. But she did so hate having a cold, for it made her nose red and her eyes water. So, looking rather brave and pathetic, she smiled wanly at Mam'zelle, and walked from the classroom.

Matron was scolding a rather sullen looking first former when Bonnie found her in the San, saying in her brisk, no-nonsense voice, 'Come now, Ruth, don't be such a baby! The sooner you take your medicine, the sooner you can get out of here and go back to your class.'

Just then, Bonnie gave another loud sneeze, and

Matron turned sharply, saying, 'Goodness me, not another one with this troublesome summer cold that's going round! Well, Bonnie, perhaps you can set an example to young Ruth here, and take a dose of medicine without complaining.'

'Of course, Matron,' said Bonnie, glancing at Ruth, who looked as if she was about to burst into tears at any second. Bonnie didn't feel very happy either, but she certainly wasn't going to let herself, or her form, down by making a fuss in front of a first former.

So Bonnie swallowed the spoonful of medicine that Matron gave her in one gulp, even managing not to grimace at the unpleasant taste.

'Not too bad at all,' she said, smiling at Ruth. 'Do you know, I think that I feel better already.'

Heartened by this, Ruth screwed up her courage and also swallowed a spoonful of the medicine, but she failed to hide her disgust as well as Bonnie had, and screwed up her face.

'Here,' said Matron, reaching into a big glass jar on her desk. 'Have a barley sugar to take the taste away.'

Ruth accepted the sweet eagerly, and went off back to her class, while Bonnie said to Matron, 'Aren't you going to offer me a barley sugar, Matron?'

'Certainly not!' cried Matron. 'I keep them for the younger girls, but certainly don't hand them out to fifth formers.'

Then her face creased into a smile, and she said, 'Oh, very well, Bonnie. As you helped me get Ruth to take her medicine, I suppose you have earned one.'

Matron handed the girl a sweet, and that was when Bonnie noticed something very strange indeed. Something that shocked her so much that she could hardly believe her eyes. For Matron's fingers were speckled with glitter!

A shock for Bonnie

Bonnie felt so stunned that, afterwards, she was quite unable to remember saying goodbye to Matron, or walking back to the classroom. But, somehow, she found herself back at her desk, suddenly aware that everyone was looking at her in concern.

'Are you all right, Bonnie?' asked Freddie anxiously. 'You look awfully pale.'

Mam'zelle, too, was worried about her favourite, and cried, 'Ah, what is Matron thinking of to send you back to your lesson in this state? You should be in bed, in the San!'

'Oh no, I am quite all right, Mam'zelle,' said Bonnie, pulling herself together. 'It's just that the medicine Matron gave me tasted so very horrid that it quite upset me.'

Mam'zelle seemed satisfied with this explanation, and Bonnie did her very best to concentrate, though it was very difficult. How on earth was she to tell the fifth form that their kindly, beloved Matron was a thief? And would they even believe her?

At break-time Bonnie dragged a very surprised Amy into a corner of the courtyard and, having looked all around to make sure that they could not be overheard, said in a low voice, 'I have something to tell you.'

'I knew that something was wrong when you came back from seeing Matron,' said Amy, with satisfaction. 'What is it?'

And then Amy listened, open-mouthed, as her friend told of her shocking discovery. Amy had no great liking for Matron, who had quickly sized her up as vain and spoilt, but even she found it almost impossible to believe that she was a thief.

'Bonnie, you simply *must* have made a mistake,' she said at last. 'Heaven knows Matron is not my favourite person, but no one could doubt her honesty.'

'Well, that's what I thought,' said Bonnie rather sadly, for she had always had a soft spot for the no-nonsense, yet kindly, Matron. 'But I saw the glitter on her hands with my own eyes.'

'Well, you will have a hard job convincing the others that Matron is a thief,' said Amy heavily. 'They all think that she is too wonderful for words.'

'I know,' sighed Bonnie. 'Even though I saw the evidence I only half believe it myself. I shall have to tell the others. I shan't accuse Matron, or say that she could be the thief. I shall simply say that she had glitter on her hands, which is the truth, and I shall leave it to the fifth formers to reach their own conclusions.'

'I suppose that is the best thing to do,' said Amy. 'When will you tell them?'

'This evening, when we are all together in the common-room,' said Bonnie. 'It's going to be jolly unpleasant, so I'd rather get it over with as soon as possible.'

So, when the fifth formers gathered in the common-room that evening, Bonnie looked round to make sure that everyone was present. There was the usual buzz of chatter, some of the girls listening to music on the radiogram, others reading and all of them looking happy and contented. Except for Bonnie, who was miserably aware that she was soon about to wipe the smiles from their faces. The girl had wracked her brains throughout the day to think of another explanation as to why Matron's fingers had been speckled with glitter, but hadn't been able to come up with anything.

She cleared her throat rather nervously now, and was just about to ask for everyone's attention when someone rapped smartly at the door. Then it was pushed open and Matron herself entered.

As the girls made to get to their feet, she said in her usual, brisk way, 'Stay where you are, girls. No need to get up, for what I have to say will only take a moment. This morning, just after you went down to breakfast, I did a quick inspection of your dormitory.'

'Heavens, Matron,' said Pam, looking alarmed. 'Don't say that someone forgot to make her bed.'

'No, I am pleased to say that everything was as neat as a new pin,' said Matron. 'Exactly as I should expect from fifth formers. There was only one thing out of place, and it was this.'

Matron reached into the big pocket of her starched, white apron and pulled something out. She stretched out her hand, and Bonnie and Amy exchanged startled glances, for in her palm lay something which sparkled and glittered.

'My brooch!' cried Bonnie.

'Ah, it *is* yours!' said Matron, handing it to Bonnie. 'I wondered if it might be, for I found it on the floor, in between your bed and Amy's.'

So that was what had happened, thought Bonnie. The brooch must have fallen on to the floor, and while the girls were making their way downstairs, Matron had done a quick dormitory inspection, and her sharp eyes had spotted it. In the time it had taken Bonnie to realise she had forgotten her handkerchief and walk back upstairs to fetch it, Matron had pocketed the brooch and made her way back to her own quarters.

'I should have asked you about the brooch when you came to my room earlier, but it went right out of my mind,' said Matron. 'Here you are, and take better care of it from now on, Bonnie.'

She handed the brooch over, then looked down at her hands, saying, 'My goodness, how the glitter comes off! I shall have to go and wash my hands now.'

Bonnie sighed with relief as the door shut behind Matron, then Pam came over and said in a low voice, 'So Matron had your brooch all along! I quite thought the thief had taken the bait, but now it seems that we are just as much in the dark as ever.'

'Yes, and I have this horrid little brooch back,' said Bonnie, sounding glum. 'I wonder if I shall ever get rid of it?'

Bonnie was unusually quiet and lost in thought for the rest of the evening, as she occupied herself with her sewing. Normally she and Amy would chatter together as she worked, but tonight Bonnie didn't seem to have much to say for herself. At last the silence grew too much for Amy, and she said, 'Whatever is the matter with you, Bonnie? I should have thought that you would have been pleased to learn that Matron isn't the thief.'

'Of course I'm pleased,' said Bonnie. 'But you know, Amy, I really don't feel awfully pleased with *myself* at the moment. You see, I knew, in my heart, that Matron would never steal anything from any of us girls. But because I had seen the evidence – or what I *thought* was evidence – I was prepared to ignore my better judgement and forget everything that I know to be true about Matron's character. It just goes to show that it's best to have faith in what you believe.'

Amy was much struck by this, and looked at her little friend with new respect, for Bonnie sounded so wise and knowledgeable.

'I really feel that I have learned something very important today,' said Bonnie, a very solemn look in her big, brown eyes. 'And it is something that I shall never forget.'

But someone who didn't seem to have learned anything in her dealings with people was Millicent.

She held another orchestra rehearsal on Saturday afternoon, and this time things went badly wrong.

Millicent was not in the best of moods, for she had planned to start the rehearsal at two o'clock, but had had to put it off until after tea.

This was thanks to June, who had already put Gillian down for tennis practice at two o'clock, and flatly refused to change it. Millicent did her best to convince Gillian that it was far more important to rehearse for the competition than play tennis, but her efforts were in vain, for Gillian said firmly, 'I can't let June down, Millicent. She put me down for tennis practice before you arranged the rehearsal, you know. But I don't want to let you down either, so if you can just hold the rehearsal later I can attend both.'

Millicent had done this, but with very bad grace indeed. Somehow the girls always seemed to feel more tired and less attentive after tea, and Millicent knew that they would not be at their best.

Her temper was not improved when she entered the hall to overhear Anne talking to Belinda.

'I think it's jolly brave of you to take Jessie's place,' Anne was saying. 'The rest of us who have been in the orchestra from the start didn't know what we were letting ourselves in for when we put our names down. But now word of Millicent's bad temper and high-handed manner has got around, so you *do* know. And you still let her talk you into it!'

Belinda gave a rather nervous laugh, and said, 'I'm not sure whether I am being brave or foolish, but no doubt I shall soon find out.'

Just then the two girls heard a loud cough behind them, and turned, startled, to see that Millicent had come in. Both of them turned red, hoping devoutly that the girl hadn't heard what they were saying.

But, as the rehearsal went on, it became clear that Millicent *had* heard.

So, Anne thought that she was bad-tempered and high-handed, and had tried to turn the new cello player against her! Well, she was in for a shock.

And, much to the surprise of the orchestra, Millicent was sweetness itself to Belinda, although the girl played a great many wrong notes.

'You have only had a few days in which to learn the music,' she said kindly. 'I am sure that you will be quite as good as Jessie was, once you have practised a little more.'

Anne, however, came in for a great deal of criticism, much of it unfair. Millicent felt very sore with Anne, for she thought it most improper of her to have spoken disrespectfully to one of the younger girls. This was very true, and Anne was regretting having done so. In fact, she had already made up her mind to go up to Millicent and apologise to her after the rehearsal. But that was before Millicent decided to humiliate her in front of the entire orchestra, and in a very short time all of Anne's good intentions had vanished.

When Millicent made her play the same passage over and over again, Anne suddenly decided that nothing, not making her parents proud, not even winning the competition for the glory of Malory Towers, was worth putting up with this for.

Deliberately, and with great relish, Anne brought her hands down hard on the keys, making a loud, discordant sound that caused the others to wince and cover their ears. Then she played the passage through for the final time, her face perfectly serious as she purposely struck all the wrong keys. The noise that Anne made was quite dreadful, but her expression and attitude were so solemn, as though she were some great concert pianist, that the others couldn't stop laughing.

Millicent listened as though she couldn't believe her ears, at first, then, when she realised that Anne was fooling, she flew into a fine rage!

'Anne, stop that at once!' she cried, quite white with anger. 'You are making a mockery of the whole thing!'

But Anne took no notice and carried on playing – and the rest of the orchestra carried on laughing!

Of course, this was really very childish behaviour from a fifth former, and Anne realised this, but there was just something about Millicent that made one *want* to behave childishly!

At last the music – if one could call it music, thought Millicent – came to an end. Anne's fingers became still on the keys, and the laughter of the rest of the orchestra ebbed away as they looked at Millicent standing before them, silent and furious.

But the girl wasn't silent for long.

'Fine behaviour for a fifth former, I must say!' she

said, her voice quivering with anger. 'And a fine example to set the younger members of the orchestra. In fact, Anne, I shall have to consider whether I can allow you back after this.'

'Oh, really?' said Anne in rather a haughty manner. 'Well, let me save you the trouble, Millicent. I wouldn't carry on playing in your beastly orchestra for the world!'

Gillian, who hadn't joined in the others' laughter at Anne's antics, stepped in to say, 'Anne, please think carefully. If you have a bone to pick with Millicent that is between the two of you, but by resigning you are letting down the orchestra and the whole school.'

'Well, you would say that, Gillian!' retorted Anne. 'Millicent never picks on you as she does on me, for you are her favourite and can do no wrong in her eyes. No, I am sorry, but my mind is made up.'

'Very well, then, go,' said Millicent, coldly.

'I shall,' said Anne, getting up from the piano and stalking towards the door. 'Do you know, I believe that I might take up tennis, instead. It will be a pleasant change to spend time with someone like June, who has the qualities that make a good leader.'

This was an unfortunate remark, for Millicent, who felt intensely jealous of June, and the way that she inspired such loyalty among the girls, bristled. And, although she did not betray it, Millicent felt extremely alarmed as Anne walked out. It had been difficult enough to replace Kathy and Jessie, but finding a good pianist at this late stage would be almost impossible.

Then Millicent suddenly remembered that Anne hadn't been her first choice. Young Hannah had, but that beastly June had got in first and nabbed her for the tennis team. Well, thought Millicent, with sudden resolve, she was going to jolly well change Hannah's mind, and get her to drop tennis and play for the orchestra instead. That would be one in the eye for June, and for Anne, too, when she saw how well the orchestra was doing without her, and how much better Hannah was.

Millicent looked round at the orchestra now. Some of them looked apprehensive, some gleeful. The girl knew that she was not going to get anything worth listening to out of them now, and decided to abandon the rehearsal for the time being. Far better, she thought, to concentrate her efforts on getting a really first-class pianist. That would give everyone's spirits a boost!

All of the girls were pleased to finish early, no one more so than Gillian. She had come straight to rehearsal from a very energetic tennis practice, and felt quite exhausted. And very soon it would be time for prep! Ah well, at least there was time for a quiet sit-down in the common-room first.

Millicent, meanwhile, was lucky enough to bump into Hannah in the corridor, and lost no time in trying to win the girl round.

'Hannah,' she said. 'I have been meaning to congratulate you on getting into the tennis team. You must be very proud.'

Hannah, who knew that Millicent had been

displeased with her for turning down a place in the orchestra, was rather taken aback by this, and stammered, 'W-why, thank you, Millicent.'

'My loss is June's gain,' said Millicent with a laugh. 'I do hope that she isn't working you too hard.'

'Oh no,' said Hannah, her eyes shining. 'June is simply marvellous, always offering help and encouragement so that somehow one wants to do one's best for her. It doesn't seem like hard work at all.'

Once again Millicent felt the familiar stab of jealousy, but she quelled it, saying brightly, 'How nice! I like to think that I have instilled the same spirit into my orchestra.'

Hannah, who, along with the rest of the school, had heard the tales of Millicent's autocratic attitude and bursts of temper, rather doubted this, but didn't dare say so.

'I may as well tell you this, Hannah,' said Millicent, leaning forward in a confidential manner. 'For you are sure to hear it sooner or later. I have had to ask Anne to resign her place in the orchestra.'

This was *almost* true, thought Millicent, for she had told Anne that she would have to consider whether she could have her back or not.

Hannah, of course, felt enormously flattered at being confided in by one of the bigger girls and, her eyes growing big, said, 'Heavens, Millicent! Whatever will you do now, without a pianist?'

'Well, between you and me, Hannah, Anne simply

wasn't up to the job,' said Millicent with a sigh. 'I decided that if I couldn't have a first-rate pianist I would rather have no one at all. Of course, it means that I am going to have to do an awful lot of rewriting, but that can't be helped.'

The girl paused for a moment, as though thinking deeply, then said, 'What a pity that you can't do as Gillian is doing, and play tennis for June, and the piano for me. Still, I suppose there aren't many girls who have Gillian's energy and commitment.'

Just then a group of Hannah's friends came along, so Millicent said goodbye and went on her way. She judged that she had said quite enough to set Hannah thinking, anyway. Millicent knew that the girl had a competitive streak, and wouldn't relish being unfavourably compared to Gillian. Really, Millicent thought, she had been quite clever in the way she had handled the situation. Hannah was sure to want to prove herself, and would soon come running to Millicent almost begging for a place in the orchestra. All she had to do was sit back and wait!

Delia makes a discovery

Millicent was quite right, for her words brought Hannah's competitive streak to the fore. The second former watched Gillian at tennis practice, a few days later, and noticed that the girl seemed to be a little off her game. She also overheard Felicity saying to June, 'Gillian really doesn't look at all well. I wouldn't be a bit surprised if she's suffering from exhaustion.'

'Oh, don't be so melodramatic!' June had scoffed. 'She's just a little tired, that's all. A good, long sleep tonight and she will be absolutely fine.'

Felicity wasn't so sure, and nor was Hannah. She began to think that it would be quite a feather in her cap if she, a mere second former, could succeed where a fifth former had failed.

So, after tea, Hannah went in search of Millicent and told her that she would be happy to play the piano for her. Millicent, of course, was thrilled and made a great fuss of Hannah, which pleased the girl enormously. So much, in fact, that she began to get a little swollen-headed and, when she returned to the second-form common-room, couldn't resist boasting a little.

'It's difficult to be so much in demand,' she said, with

a little toss of her head. 'But both June and Millicent are relying on me, so I must do my best not to let them down. Or the school, of course, for I am doing all of this for the honour of Malory Towers.'

The downright second formers, however, weren't fooled by this, and Hilda, the head-girl, said scornfully, 'Pooh! You're doing this for your own glory, my girl. You like the idea that you are "in demand", as you call it, and are enjoying setting two of the fifth formers at loggerheads.'

'What nonsense!' said Hannah, though her cheeks turned a little pink. 'Besides, June and Millicent aren't at loggerheads. How can they be, when June doesn't even know yet that I am going to be in the orchestra.'

'Oho!' cried Hilda. 'So June doesn't know yet? Well, she's going to be none too pleased when she finds out, you mark my words!'

Hilda was quite right. Millicent took great delight, that evening, in telling June that Hannah was going to play piano in the orchestra. June was very displeased, for, although she would not admit it to any of the others, she had seen the toll that being involved in both projects was taking on Gillian. She had held her tongue, for she had hoped that Gillian would see sense and resign from the orchestra. But gradually she had come to realise that Gillian was the kind of person who stuck to her word and, if she said that she would do a thing, jolly well did it! And now here was one of the younger girls – and another of her star players – trying to copy her!

June had no intention of letting Millicent see that she was annoyed, though, and said with a smile, 'I hope that she works as hard for you as she does for me, Millicent. I know that you have a talent for getting the best out of people. People like Kathy, and Jessie, and Anne . . . oh no, wait a minute! They have all resigned from the orchestra, haven't they? Well, Hannah is a sticker, just like Gillian, so at least you know that you have two players you can rely on.'

Millicent's face darkened, and June laughed softly, before saying, 'Be careful, Millicent, or your entry for the competition might just be a duet, instead of an orchestra!'

So Millicent was the one left feeling cross and uncomfortable, and she stomped away, wondering bitterly how it was that she never managed to get the better of June when they had one of their clashes.

As soon as she was out of earshot, June turned to Freddie, who was sitting beside her and had overheard the whole exchange, saying determinedly, 'She's not having Hannah. And I shall get Gillian away from her somehow, too. They are two of my best players, and I don't like to see them splitting themselves in two, so to speak.'

'But what can you do?' asked Freddie. 'You can hardly order them to resign from the orchestra. And if you make them choose, there is always the chance that they might choose Millicent.'

'I know,' said June, with a sigh. 'And I can't risk that,

for without them Malory Towers hasn't a hope of winning the tennis tournament.'

'Perhaps you and Millicent could reach a compromise,' suggested Freddie. 'You could have Gillian, and she could have Hannah, or vice-versa. At least then you both end up with someone first-rate.'

But June was far too stubborn to agree to any kind of compromise, and she was quite certain that Millicent was too.

In fact, both girls were far more alike than they cared to admit. June was firmly convinced that her tennis tournament was far more important than Millicent's little competition. And Millicent thought that tennis was just a silly game, unlike music, which was lasting and brought pleasure to so many people.

One thing the two girls did have in common was their determination to bring glory to their school. Freddie, glancing from one to the other, thought that if they had both been on the same side they would have been a formidable force indeed. What a pity that they were enemies instead!

Millicent slept well that night, for she decided that it was foolish to let June needle her. Instead, she decided to think of the good things that had happened that day. She had lost Anne, but had got Hannah – the girl she had really wanted – in her place. The youngster was going to have to put in a lot of practice to learn the music in time, but that was good too, for it meant that she would have less time to spend on tennis. And June wouldn't like that at all!

June took a little longer to get to sleep, for she was turning over various plans in her mind to get Gillian and Hannah to leave the orchestra and concentrate solely on their tennis. Hannah would be relatively easy, she decided, for the girl admired her, June, enormously. All she had to do was take an interest in one of the other youngsters, and hint that Hannah's place in the team was at risk if she spent too much time rehearsing with the orchestra. Hannah would soon fall into line, for she thought a great deal more of June's good opinion than she did of Millicent's. Once she had arrived at this decision, June felt a lot easier in her mind and soon dropped off.

Very soon all the fifth formers were asleep – apart from one. Poor Delia was feeling very troubled, for that very morning she had received a letter from Gillian's mother. Mrs Weaver had written:

I was quite concerned when I saw how ill Gillian looked at half-term. I feel so much happier now that I know that Gillian has a good friend, who will watch over her and make sure that she won't overdo things.

But although Delia had watched over Gillian, she hadn't been able to stop her from doing exactly as she pleased. Sometimes Delia would broach the subject, rather tentatively, but Gillian would always brush it aside, her manner becoming bright as she insisted that she was quite well and enjoyed having plenty to occupy her time. And Delia wasn't a strong enough character to push the matter. She sat up in bed suddenly, hugging her knees. A shaft of moonlight shone through a crack in the curtains, and she could see all of the fifth formers asleep in their beds. Delia sighed softly, wondering what the others would do in her position. If Felicity was worried about Susan, she would tell her so, straight out, thought Delia. She certainly wouldn't allow herself to be brushed off, and nor would Susan if anything was the matter with Felicity. It was the same with Pam and Nora, Julie and Lucy, and Amy and Bonnie.

None of them would be afraid of taking the bull by the horns, even if it meant the risk of causing offence, or falling out. Because they knew that their friendships would survive, and even grow stronger as a result. That was the trouble, thought Delia. She was too afraid of pushing Gillian away altogether, and losing her. But then, if she could lose her so easily, perhaps their friendship wasn't worth having.

With these thoughts churning around in her head, Delia lay down again and, at last, fell into an uneasy and fitful doze. A sound woke her, some hours later, and her eyes flew open. Blinking, she sat up and saw that the door was opening, a dark shape silhouetted there. In the middle of the night, all sorts of horrid, creepy thoughts filled Delia's mind, and she wondered if she should yell, and wake the others. Then the shape closed the door and advanced into the room, and Delia felt weak with relief as the shaft of moonlight fell on it, and she realised that it was only Gillian.

She must have been to the bathroom, thought Delia,

and whispered, 'Gillian! Are you all right?'

But Gillian had climbed back into bed and gone straight off to sleep again. Which, thought Delia, just proved how exhausted she was.

The girl mentioned the incident to Gillian the following morning, as they dressed.

Gillian laughed, and said, 'Heavens, I must have been worn out, for I don't remember getting out of bed at all! Why, I must have gone to the bathroom in my sleep.'

'You always seem worn out these days,' said Delia. 'And I can't say I'm surprised.'

Once again Gillian laughed, and brushed her friend's words aside, but this time Delia was determined not to let the matter drop so easily. She opened her mouth to speak, but before she could do so, Freddie suddenly cried, 'I say! The thief has struck again! I bought myself a new hair-slide when I went into town the other day, and it has completely vanished.'

'Are you sure it hasn't just fallen on the floor, as Bonnie's brooch did the other day?' asked Felicity. 'I know how careless you are with your things, Freddie.'

'No, for I put it in the drawer of my cabinet when I took it out last night,' said Freddie.

'That's right,' said June. 'I saw you.'

'It seems that our thief is getting desperate,' said Amy with a sniff. 'First she goes for purses, and things like watches and brooches – not to mention my expensive perfume – and now all she can find to take is a cheap hair-slide.'

'Do you mind?' said Freddie. 'It might just be a cheap hair-slide to you, Amy, but I spent the last of my pocket money on it. What's more, I don't have another one, and Miss James will probably send me out of the class for having untidy hair.'

Fortunately Felicity was able to prevent this disaster from befalling Freddie, by lending her a hair-slide of her own. But the most recent theft put everything else out of the girls' heads for the moment, and the chance for Delia to tackle Gillian was lost.

Pam was very concerned, for as head of the form she felt that it was up to her to do her utmost to catch the thief, or at least stop her, and so far her efforts had met with no success at all.

'If Freddie put her hair-slide in her drawer, that means that it must have been taken overnight, when we were all asleep,' she said. 'Right from under our very noses. And yet not one of us woke up and saw or heard a thing.'

'Perhaps it isn't someone from our form at all,' suggested Susan. 'It could be someone from another dormitory sneaking in here, and into our common-room.'

'Well, I suppose that's possible,' said Pam. 'Though I can't think who would have such a grudge against the fifth form. I have made a decision though. If the thief hasn't slipped up and been caught by the end of the week, I am going to Miss Grayling.'

No one felt very happy about this, for the girls always liked to deal with such matters themselves, if they could.

But they were forced to admit defeat on this occasion, and agree that there was nothing else they could do.

Delia, meanwhile, was very thoughtful, and very troubled. For she *had* woken up, and she had seen something. She had seen Gillian, out of her bed. But the girl had been nowhere near Freddie's cabinet. In fact, she had been coming into the dormitory from the landing. Ah yes, said a troublesome little voice in Delia's head, but suppose Gillian had already taken Freddie's hair-slide before you woke up? Suppose that she hadn't been to the bathroom at all, but had gone out to hide the hair-slide somewhere, before slipping back in? Determinedly, Delia hushed the voice. How could she even think such a thing about her best friend? And then, the little voice piped up again, there was the business of Millicent's notebook being in Gillian's bag. But Delia had never asked for an explanation. Perhaps if she had done so at the time, Gillian would have been able to clear the matter up, and these horrible doubts wouldn't keep popping up.

'Horrid, isn't it?' said a voice in her ear suddenly, making her jump. Delia turned to find Gillian standing behind her.

'I say, are you all right?' asked Gillian, frowning. 'You look awfully serious.'

'Oh, I was just thinking about all these thefts,' said Delia, turning a little red. 'That's enough to make anyone look serious!'

'Yes, that's just what I was saying,' said Gillian. 'Poor

Freddie! I know that she hasn't lost anything valuable, but it must feel horrible to think that someone has been in your drawer, and gone through all your belongings. Ugh! It quite gives me the creeps.'

Delia was cheered by this, for surely Gillian couldn't have spoken with such conviction if she really had been the thief. Smiling, she slipped her arm through the girl's, and said, 'Let's try to put it out of our minds for a while. Ah, there's the breakfast bell. I'm starving!'

'Me too,' said Gillian. 'I shall need a good breakfast, for I mean to get some extra tennis practice in this afternoon. I was quite off my game yesterday.'

'Perhaps you were off your game because you have been practising *too* hard,' suggested Delia rather timidly as they made their way downstairs.

'There's no such thing as practising too hard,' said Gillian, pulling a wry face. 'When it comes to tennis or music, it really is a case of practice makes perfect.'

'Of course,' said Delia. 'But surely even the most dedicated sportswoman or musician needs some time to relax.'

'You're absolutely right,' said Gillian, and Delia felt her heart lift. Then it sank again, as Gillian added, 'And the time to relax is when the tournament and the orchestra competition are both over. Ah, you wait, Delia, you will see a different side to me then, I promise you. I shall become so lazy that I'll make Nora look positively energetic.'

Perhaps, thought Delia, Gillian really did know best

after all. She seemed quite cheerful this morning, and the dark shadows beneath her eyes were less pronounced, although she had had a disturbed night. When June heard that she was planning to get some extra tennis practice in, she patted Gillian on the back and exclaimed, 'That's what I like to see! A bit of enthusiasm. Good for you, Gillian.'

And, in Delia's mind, that settled it. Everyone said what a marvellous games captain June was, and the whole school knew how well she looked after her players. So if June thought it was all right for Gillian to keep up the pace she had set herself, it must be.

The lower school were also having tennis practice that day, and June made a point of singling out Barbara, the reserve. She praised the girl extravagantly, applauding her every shot, so that Barbara soon began to feel quite overwhelmed. Poor Hannah, on the other hand, found herself almost ignored, though she was practising very hard indeed and really playing very well.

After her game had finished, Hannah, feeling rather hurt, went up to June and said hesitantly, 'June, have I offended you in some way?'

'Of course not,' said June brightly. 'What makes you think that, Hannah?'

'Well, it's just that I played my very hardest today, yet you didn't even seem to notice.'

'I did notice,' said June. 'And of course I am very pleased. But you see, Hannah, I have decided that I need to pay more attention to Barbara, as it is likely that she will be playing in one of the matches now. She is not as good as you, and doesn't have your confidence.'

'Barbara may be playing in one of the matches?' said Hannah, not liking the sound of this. 'I don't understand, June. I thought that she was to be reserve.'

'Yes, she is. But now that you have decided to play in Millicent's orchestra, I have to be prepared for the fact that you may find it too much,' said June.

'Oh, but I shan't!' said Hannah, dismayed. 'Really, June, I wouldn't have taken it on if I had thought it would be too much for me.'

'I'm quite sure that you wouldn't,' said June with a smile. 'But you see, Hannah, the responsibility of choosing the best players for the team doesn't lie with you. It lies with me. And if *I* think that your commitment to the orchestra is interfering with your tennis, then I may have no choice but to replace you.'

Poor Hannah felt so upset that she could barely speak. Why, she had written to her parents and grand-parents to tell them that she was playing in the tournament, and they had written back, all of them telling her how proud they were. If June were to drop her now it would be too bad!

'Cheer up, Hannah,' said June. 'I haven't dropped you yet. And even if I do, why, you will still have the honour of playing in the orchestra. Of course, you will just be one of many, and the real glory – if you win – will be Millicent's. Now, if you were to win your tennis match, it would be your victory, and yours alone.'

Clever June gave Hannah a few moments to digest this, then she called out, 'Oh, jolly well played, Barbara! Hannah, do excuse me, while I go and speak to Barbara.'

Hannah was left alone, and she thought hard. June's words had hit home, as the girl had known they would. The honour of the school was very important, but how marvellous it would be to have a slice of the glory all to herself, thought Hannah. And, if she won her singles match, that is what she would have. She glanced across at Barbara, who was hanging on June's every word, staring up at her with an adoring expression. Oh, she simply couldn't bear it if the girl took her place on the team, and got what she so badly wanted herself! Hannah's mind was made up. Now came the difficult bit – informing Millicent of her decision!

A most peculiar night

The atmosphere in the fifth-form class-room was not at all pleasant during prep that evening. As Lucy remarked to Julie, 'You could cut the air with a knife.'

The reason, of course, was that Hannah had told Millicent of her decision not to play piano in the orchestra after all. Millicent had been simply furious, and had been very cold indeed to Hannah.

June, on the other hand, was delighted when Hannah sought her out and told her that she had decided to devote herself to tennis.

'I'm very pleased to hear it,' June had said with a wide smile. 'I didn't relish the idea of losing one of my best players to Millicent. I feel sure that you have made the right decision, Hannah. But then, I always knew that you would, for you're a very bright kid.'

These words of praise were very pleasant to hear, and Hannah felt more convinced than ever that she had been right to leave the orchestra, though she still felt a little upset at letting Millicent down.

The next person to seek June out was Millicent. She found her down by the tennis courts, along with Felicity, Susan, Freddie and Gillian, and all five girls knew from the expression on Millicent's face that she was in a temper.

The girl wasted no time in getting to the point, saying angrily, 'You mean beast, June! How dare you lure Hannah away from me?'

'Lure?' repeated June, with a soft laugh. 'Let me assure you, my dear Millicent, there was no luring necessary. Hannah is quite capable of reaching her own decision, and that is exactly what she did.'

'Yes, with a little help from you, no doubt,' snapped Millicent. 'You are determined to sabotage my efforts to win the orchestra competition.'

'Oh, don't talk nonsense,' said June, beginning to lose patience now. 'I hope that you do win the competition, but not at the cost of my tennis tournament.'

'Well, I'm hardly likely to win without a pianist,' said Millicent bitterly. 'In fact, we might as well pull out.'

'Come now, Millicent,' said Felicity, beginning to feel a little sorry for the girl. 'There are several girls in the school who can play piano, and I'm sure that there is still time for someone to learn the music. You'll find someone.'

'Yes, someone third-rate,' said Millicent bitterly. 'Hannah and Anne were by far the best players in the school.'

'And you've lost them both,' said June, in a light drawl that made Millicent long to shake her.

Just then Pam came up, and seeing Millicent's angry expression and June's mocking one, her heart sank.

'What's up?' she asked, dreading the answer.

But Millicent's eyes suddenly lit up, and she almost pounced on Pam, seizing her arm.

'Hey!' shouted Pam. 'Steady on, Millicent!'

'Sorry,' said Millicent, slackening her grip. 'Pam, I've just remembered that you play the piano. How would you like to be in the orchestra?'

'Good idea,' said June, with a grin. 'Pam, Millicent was just saying that she was looking for a third-rate pianist!'

'June, do be quiet!' said Felicity, seeing that Millicent looked as if she was about to explode again. But the girl calmed herself and said evenly, 'Actually, I said that I feared I might have to make do with a third-rate pianist. Then I remembered you, Pam. Do say that you will do it.'

Pam looked into Millicent's intense, earnest face and saw at once how much the competition meant to her.

'Very well,' she said at last. 'I will do it, for the sake of the school. But please understand this, Millicent. I will not be bullied or humiliated by you. Any of that kind of thing, and I shall resign at once. Is that clear?'

'Absolutely,' said Millicent, feeling very relieved indeed. Pam wasn't the best pianist in the school, but she was better than no one. And perhaps Millicent could re-write things a little, so that she didn't have quite such a complicated solo to learn.

'Well, all has ended happily,' said June, smiling. 'Millicent has found her third-rate pianist, and Pam has the satisfaction of knowing that she was only third choice.'

Millicent shot June a poisonous glare and stalked off,

while Pam said amiably, 'You know, June, if we weren't in the fifth form I would scrag you.'

June laughed at this, while Susan said, 'I hope you know what you've let yourself in for, Pam.'

The easygoing Pam shrugged, and said, 'Well, it's as I said to Millicent. Any nonsense and I shall clear off. How do you find her, Gillian?'

'Well, I know that she can be very harsh to some of the others,' said Gillian. 'But she's never been unpleasant to me.'

'No, because she is afraid that you will leave her high and dry,' said June. 'And she can't afford to lose anyone else.'

'Yes, as it is she's scraping the bottom of the barrel, having to suffer me as pianist,' said Pam drily.

'Ah well, never mind,' said June, a wicked sparkle in her eyes. 'I daresay she will tell the others to play more loudly so that they drown out all your wrong notes. Ouch, you beast! That hurt!'

The others laughed, as Pam playfully punched June in the shoulder. She really was very good-natured, thought Gillian, joining in the laughter. Then, all of a sudden, a great wave of tiredness seemed to wash over her, as it often did these days, and she put a hand over her mouth to stifle a yawn.

'An early night for me tonight, I think,' she said.

'I should think so,' said Pam. 'I went past one of the music-rooms last night and heard you practising until almost ten o'clock. You were singing, too. I must

173

say, you have the most beautiful voice.'

Gillian looked puzzled for a moment. She hadn't been singing, and she certainly didn't have a beautiful voice – far from it! Then she remembered that Delia had been with her, and had sung along to the music. The girl had added some more words to the little song she had written and had wanted to see how they sounded. And they had sounded fine, sung in Delia's melodic, lilting voice. But Delia still firmly refused to believe that she had any talent at all, and Gillian knew that she would not want the others to know that it was she who had been singing.

So she said, quite truthfully, 'Oh, my voice is nothing special, Pam.'

'You're too modest,' said Pam. 'You really must sing for the girls in the common-room one evening.'

'Perhaps,' said Gillian, making up her mind to develop a sore throat at the earliest opportunity.

Gillian really did feel quite exhausted, and she surprised the others by going to bed at eight o'clock that evening.

'Heavens!' said Bonnie. 'Fancy going up to bed early when you don't have to.'

'I'll come with you,' said Delia.

'You don't have to,' said Gillian. 'Stay up and chat with the others if you want to.'

But Delia insisted that she felt tired as well, so the two girls said goodnight to the others and made their way up to the dormitory.

In fact, Delia had made a plan. She intended to get to sleep early, and wake up a few hours later, just to see if anyone did come into the dormitory and try to steal anything.

Gillian fell asleep as soon as her head touched the pillow, and as soon as she had dropped off, Delia set her little alarm clock for one in the morning and placed it under her own pillow. Of course, it might be that the thief would not strike tonight, in which case Delia was in for a long, lonely and very boring night. But that was a chance she would have to take, and if the thief did come in it would all be worth it.

Very soon Delia was asleep too, and the rest of the fifth formers were careful to make as little noise as possible when they came up a couple of hours later, so as not to disturb the sleeping girls.

Soon all was quiet, and remained so until one o'clock, when Delia's alarm clock went off. She woke at once and slipped her hand under the pillow to stop the muffled ringing. Then the girl sat up and looked round, relieved to see that no one else had heard it, for everyone was fast asleep.

Half an hour crept by very slowly indeed, and Delia wished that she had a torch, so that she might have read under the covers. At last, more for something to do than because she really wanted it, she went to the bathroom to get a glass of water. And while she was in there, she heard the unmistakable sound of footsteps on the landing. Delia waited until she heard them going downstairs, then, very softly, she opened the bathroom door and peeped out.

Yes, someone was walking down the stairs. Someone wearing spotted pyjamas, and with a very distinctive head of red hair. Gillian!

Delia's heart sank. Surely she hadn't woken up in the hope of catching the thief only for it to turn out to be her best friend? But she could think of no other reason for Gillian to be wandering around in the middle of the night. She waited for the girl to reach the bottom of the stairs, then padded soundlessly after her, keeping her distance and staying in the shadows.

Delia watched as Gillian went into the common-room, her heart thumping so loudly that she was sure the girl must be able to hear it! But Gillian was intent on whatever she was doing, and didn't so much as glance round.

Delia hid herself in an alcove just along the corridor and waited and listened. Gillian was muttering something to herself, and Delia strained to hear what it was. It sounded as if she was saying, 'Where is it? Where is it?' over and over again. How odd! What on earth could she be looking for? A few moments later Gillian emerged. She was carrying something, Delia saw, and the girl had to stop herself from gasping out loud when she saw what it was. A delicate little embroidered spectacle case that Bonnie had made for her aunt's birthday. Bonnie had only finished it last night, and had put it in her needlework box, which she kept in the common-room cupboard. But what on earth did Gillian want with it? She didn't even wear spectacles. Delia shook herself. What did that matter? What was more important, and deeply shocking, was the discovery that Gillian, her dearest friend, was the thief. Oh dear, now what was she to do?

Someone else had woken up in the fifth-form dormitory. Felicity, disturbed by a sudden, loud snore from Susan, in the next bed, had woken with a start and, after trying unsuccessfully to get back to sleep again, sat up and rubbed her eyes. That was when she noticed that two of the beds were empty. One was Delia's, but whose was the other? Oh yes, Gillian's, of course. But where on earth could the pair of them be?

Surely Gillian hadn't been so foolish as to go and practise her music at this hour, and had persuaded Delia to go with her? If one of the mistresses caught them they would be in big trouble, and it would reflect badly on the whole form.

Felicity glanced across at Pam, and debated whether to wake her. But the head-girl was sleeping so soundly that she didn't have the heart. Instead, Felicity climbed out of bed, put on her slippers and decided to try and track down the absentees herself.

Fortunately she didn't have far to go, for when she got downstairs she could see Gillian quite clearly. But what on earth was she doing?

Under the stairs was a big cupboard, which was used for storing all sorts of odds and ends. Gillian had opened the door, and appeared to be putting something in there, Felicity saw, feeling completely bewildered. What very peculiar behaviour!

Delia suddenly appeared behind Gillian, so intent on what her friend was doing that she didn't even notice Felicity standing in the shadows.

Delia moved closer to Gillian, and peered into the cupboard, giving a gasp as she saw what else was in there. Nora's watch, Susan's chocolates, Amy's perfume – all the things that had been taken from the girls recently.

Poor Delia felt quite sick. How could she have been so mistaken in her reading of Gillian's character? She would have to tell the others, of course. It was only fair. Then they would all get their things back, and the form as a whole would decide what was to happen to Gillian.

'Gillian!' she hissed, standing right behind the girl. But Gillian didn't turn round. In fact, she didn't even seem to know that Delia was there at all. Instead, she was inside the cupboard, arranging all of the stolen things into a neat pile.

Felicity had been watching all this with a puzzled frown on her face, and she stepped out of the shadows, making Delia jump.

'Felicity!' she gasped. 'Oh, you did give me a fright.'

'Never mind that,' said Felicity. 'Delia, what on earth is going on here?'

'See for yourself,' said Delia sadly, indicating the pile of stolen belongings in the cupboard.

Now it was Felicity's turn to gasp, but before she could ask for an explanation, Gillian turned round, a strange smile on her face.

'I've found it,' she said. 'I just hope that I remember where I put it tomorrow.'

There was a queer, glassy look in her eyes, and she seemed to be staring straight through the two girls. It sent shivers up and down Delia's spine, and she said, 'Stop it, Gillian! You're talking nonsense.'

'Wait a minute!' said Felicity, realisation dawning on her. 'Delia, she's sleepwalking! I don't believe that Gillian knows we are here! I remember when I was in the first form, there was a girl in the dorm next door who used to do it. She came into our dorm a few times, and it was jolly frightening at first, until we realised what she was doing.'

'Oh!' said Delia, her brow clearing. 'We had better wake her up, then.'

'No, don't do that,' said Felicity quickly. 'I remember Matron telling us that you should never wake sleepwalkers. The shock can do them terrible harm.'

'Then what do we do?' asked Delia.

'We simply guide her back to bed,' said Felicity. 'You take one arm, Delia, and I will take the other.'

Gillian proved quite unresisting, and the two girls got her out of the big cupboard, then shut the door. Then they led her back upstairs and to her own bed, watching in astonishment as she climbed in, and went straight off to sleep as though nothing had happened.

'Well!' whispered Delia. 'What a very strange night this has been.'

'Very strange,' agreed Felicity in a low voice. 'And it's not over yet. Come with me, Delia.'

'Where are we going?' asked the girl.

'To the bathroom,' said Felicity. 'We need to discuss this, and I don't want to disturb the others.'

Things are cleared up

The two girls tiptoed to the bathroom and shut the door softly behind them. Then Felicity turned to Delia, and said, 'Am I to understand that Gillian took those things?'

'It looks like it, I'm afraid,' said Delia, and explained how Gillian had come out of the common-room with Bonnie's spectacle case.

'She was muttering to herself all the time she was in there,' Delia said. 'Something that sounded like, "Where is it?", over and over.'

'This is a strange business,' said Felicity. 'But there is one good thing that has come out of it.'

'Oh?' said Delia, quite unable to think what it could be.

'Of course,' said Felicity. 'Gillian must have been taking those things while she was sleepwalking. So although she is the thief, she's not *really* a thief, because she didn't know that she was stealing.'

'Yes!' said Delia, looking much happier suddenly. 'I say, Felicity, the others will see it that way too, won't they? I mean to say, they won't want to haul poor Gillian up before the Head, will they?'

'I am quite certain that they won't,' said Felicity. 'Once they know the whole story they will see that

Gillian wasn't to blame. And they will be jolly glad to get their things back, too.'

Delia seemed reassured by this, and lapsed into thoughtful silence for a few moments. At last, she said, 'Sleepwalking isn't a good thing, is it, Felicity?'

'No, it's not,' said Felicity, looking very grave. 'I believe that it usually means the sufferer is troubled about something, or is overdoing things.'

'Well, poor old Gillian has been doing far too much,' said Delia, feeling very guilty indeed. 'I just wish that I had been firmer with her, and tried harder to get her to relax. But I'm afraid I'm not very good at being firm with people.'

The girl looked so forlorn that Felicity felt touched, and she gave her a pat on the shoulder, saying, 'Well, Gillian is one of those people who sticks to a decision once she has made her mind up. You mustn't blame yourself, Delia, for people like that are very hard to move. I know that Pam tried speaking to her too, and she failed to make any impression on her.'

Felicity paused for a moment, then went on, 'But I am afraid that the sleepwalking puts a different complexion on things. Gillian must be *made* to listen to reason, and I think that we will have to call in someone in a position of authority to talk to her.'

'Miss Grayling?' said Delia, looking rather scared.

'I was actually thinking of Matron,' said Felicity. 'She has had experience in these matters, you know. I remember how well she took care of Jenny, the girl who started sleepwalking when we were in the first form.'

'Of course!' said Delia, brightening. 'Matron is just the person.'

'Well, you and I will go to her tomorrow, Delia,' said Felicity decidedly. 'She will know what to do for the best, you may be sure.'

Now that they had decided on a course of action, the two girls suddenly felt tired, and Felicity gave a yawn.

'Heavens, what a night!' she said. 'Come along, Delia, we'd better get some sleep, for it will be time to get up before we know it.'

So the two girls crept back into their dormitory, and, as Gillian had earlier, fell asleep at once.

After breakfast the following morning, there was half an hour before the first lesson began. Felicity and Delia had put their heads together in the dormitory that morning and made a plan. As soon as breakfast was over, Delia said to Gillian, 'How about a quick walk in the grounds before Maths?'

Gillian had agreed to this, and, once the two girls were out of the way, Felicity said, 'I would like you all to come with me, please. I have something to show you.'

The fifth formers were rather startled at this, and Nora said, 'What is it, Felicity? A surprise?'

'In a manner of speaking, yes,' said Felicity. 'Do come along, everyone, and you'll see.'

Felicity led the curious fifth formers to the big cupboard where Gillian had hidden their things, and she pulled open the door. There was a moment's astonished silence, then the astonished cries of the girls filled the air.

'My purse!'

'And mine! And Nora, there is your watch.'

'My perfume is here,' said Amy in delight. 'And it looks as if it hasn't been used at all.'

'Felicity, how did you discover this?' asked Pam, looking bewildered. 'Do you know how they came to be here, and who the thief is?'

'Yes, I do,' answered Felicity and, as quickly as possible, she told the others the story of how she and Delia had discovered Gillian sleepwalking last night.

As she had expected, the fifth formers were most sympathetic, and didn't blame Gillian at all for her actions.

'I just feel relieved that there is a simple explanation, and that we know there isn't a thief in the fifth form,' said Nora.

'Yes, it's a weight off all our minds,' said Freddie. 'It really was horrible feeling that there might be a thief in our midst.'

'Poor Gillian,' said Susan. 'I should think she will be absolutely mortified when she discovers that it was she who took our things – even though she did it in her sleep!'

'Well, I don't want her to find out just yet,' said Felicity. 'At break-time Delia and I are going to tell Matron about Gillian's sleepwalking, for I really feel that this is something we can't deal with ourselves.'

'Yes, you're quite right,' said Pam. 'Very well, we

shan't say a word to Gillian, and we shall all have to try and behave quite normally towards her until Matron has seen her.'

This wasn't easy, of course, for the girls felt so sorry for Gillian that they went out of their way to be extra nice to her. So much so, that the girl began to wonder what she had done to deserve it! And the two who were nicest of all were June and Millicent, for both of them felt a little guilty, knowing that it was largely their fault that Gillian was so overworked that she had begun sleepwalking.

Pam too felt a little guilty, for she had known that Gillian was tired, and doing far too much. True, she had tried to speak to Gillian about it, but when the girl brushed her concerns aside, perhaps she, Pam, as head-girl, should have gone to Matron or Miss James and let them deal with it.

At break-time Felicity and Delia went off to tell Matron the extraordinary story of Gillian's sleepwalking, though they left out the part about her taking their things. Matron listened, her expression becoming more serious as the tale went on, and when the girls had finished she said gravely, 'You did the right thing in coming to me, girls. This is a very serious matter, and must be dealt with before Gillian exhausts herself completely.'

Delia looked rather anxious, and said, 'I'm afraid that she will be angry with Felicity and me for going behind her back like this.'

'Now, don't you worry your head about that,' said Matron, kindly. 'I daresay she may feel annoyed with you at first, but once she has had a good rest and feels better, she will soon realise that you did it for her own good.' Matron got to her feet. 'Now I had better go and find Gillian, and break the news to her that she has been sleepwalking. Then I'm going to tuck her up in bed in the San.'

'She won't like that, Matron,' said Felicity.

'She won't have any say in the matter!' said Matron with a grim smile. 'I had better tell Miss Grayling all about it, as well, 'for it won't do to keep her in the dark.'

Indeed it wouldn't, for the Head took a keen interest in the welfare of all the girls, and would certainly want to be kept informed of Gillian's progress.

Gillian was very surprised when Matron approached her in the courtyard and said, 'Gillian, may I have a word with you in my room, please?'

'Of course, Matron,' said Gillian, looking rather puzzled. 'Is something the matter?'

'No, but we need to have a little talk,' Matron said, laying a firm but gentle hand on Gillian's shoulder and leading her away.

The others felt very subdued when they went into their French lesson, and Mam'zelle Dupont, noticing how listless they seemed, felt quite concerned about them, and gave the fifth formers a very easy time indeed.

Gillian did not return to class that day and, after tea, an anxious Delia went to Matron's room in search of news.

'She is sleeping now,' said Matron. 'And I'm hoping that she will go right through until morning.'

'When will she be able to come back to class, Matron?' asked Delia.

'Not for a few days, I'm afraid,' said Matron. 'And when she does, she must give up this nonsense of being in the tennis team and the school orchestra. Oh yes, I know all about that,' said Matron, smiling a little at Delia's surprised expression. 'Gillian and I had a very long talk earlier. She has known for some time that she has been overdoing things, but didn't know how to get out of it without letting either June or Millicent down. Well, the outcome is that she will have to let the pair of them down, for she is in no fit state to take on any extra activities.'

'Oh dear,' said Delia, looking very unhappy. 'I do feel that I am partly to blame for this, Matron, for I promised Gillian's mother that I would keep an eye on her. I'm afraid that I haven't done a very good job.'

'Well, I've no doubt you did your best,' said Matron, kindly. 'But you could hardly force Gillian to give up one of her commitments.'

'No, but it's jolly lucky that *you* managed to talk some sense into her,' said Delia. 'I can't think how you got her to listen to you.'

Matron laughed at this, and said drily, 'Well, Delia, I have a great many years' experience in dealing with stubborn, strong-willed girls. Gillian soon realised that she had met her match in me! Now, off you go and you may come and visit Gillian tomorrow. Tell the others that they may come too, but no more than two at a time.'

Delia went off to relay this news to the fifth formers. They were all pleased to learn that Gillian would be able to return to class in a few days, but June and Millicent were dismayed to learn that they had both lost their star player.

'But Gillian *must* play in the orchestra!' cried Millicent, a look of horror on her face. 'I simply can't manage without her. We have already had so many setbacks, and now this.'

'If that isn't just like you, Millicent,' said Felicity scornfully. 'Poor Gillian is ill, and all that you can think about is your precious orchestra.'

Millicent flushed, and said, 'Of course I'm concerned about Gillian, and I want her to get well as much as any of you. I can't help worrying about my orchestra, though.'

'And what about you, June?' said Susan. 'I suppose you're fretting about who is going to take Gillian's place in the tennis tournament.'

'Nothing of the sort,' said June, coolly. In fact, she was just as bitterly disappointed as Millicent, but was clever enough not to betray it to the others. 'Freddie is reserve, so she will take Gillian's place.'

A cheer went up at this, for everyone liked the cheerful, good-natured Freddie, and all were pleased that her chance had come to shine. Freddie herself turned quite pink with pleasure, and said, 'Now don't make me practise too hard, June, or *I* shall exhaust myself too, and end up in the San with Gillian.'

Delia, armed with a large bar of chocolate and the good wishes of the others, went off to visit Gillian the following morning. She felt a little apprehensive at first, for she was afraid that Gillian might be angry with her for going to Matron.

But, much to her relief, the girl greeted her with a warm smile, saying, 'Delia, how lovely to see you! My word, is that enormous bar of chocolate for me? How super!'

As she sat down on the edge of the bed, Delia was relieved to see that her friend looked much better after a good, long sleep, the colour beginning to return to her cheeks and the dark shadows beneath her eyes much less pronounced.

The two girls chatted about this and that for a while, then Delia said, rather hesitantly, 'Gillian, I do hope that you aren't annoyed with me for speaking to Matron about you. But I really was awfully worried, and didn't know what else to do.'

'Well, I was a bit cross with you at first,' admitted Gillian. 'But now that I feel well rested I am seeing things more clearly, and realise that you have done me a favour. I had begun to see that I was overdoing things, but I've always been a sticker, and couldn't bring myself to say to either June or Millicent that I wanted to pull out. I thought that everyone would think I was weak, and couldn't keep to my word. But then you and Felicity caught me sleepwalking, and once Matron told me what I had been doing, I knew that I simply couldn't go on like this without making myself really ill. You're a jolly good friend, Delia.'

'Thanks,' said Delia, rather gruffly. 'I only wish that I had been firmer with you earlier on. Your mother asked me to keep an eye on you, you know, at half-term. I feel as if I've let her down a bit.'

'Nothing of the sort,' said Gillian, putting her hand over Delia's. 'It was all my own stupid fault for not taking any notice of you. I knew what you were trying to do, in your own gentle way, but I was so sure that I knew what was best for me, I just brushed your worries aside. And you are so lacking in confidence that you let me.'

This was certainly true, and Delia nodded.

'Well,' said Gillian, 'from now on, if you have anything to say to me I want you to tell me straight. Even shout at me, if need be, and, even if I don't agree with what you say, I shall take notice of you!'

'I don't know if I shall shout,' laughed Delia. 'But I shall certainly tell you what's on my mind. Which reminds me, we have cleared up that business of the fifth-form thief.'

'Really?' said Gillian, her eyes growing wide. 'Who was it?'

'Well, the thing is, Gillian,' said Delia, 'it was you.'

Gillian, of course, looked completely taken aback, and, quickly, Delia rushed on, 'You didn't take things intentionally. We all know that you would never do that.

But you were doing it while you were sleepwalking. Felicity and I caught you in the act.'

And Delia explained everything to an astonished Gillian, who listened open-mouthed.

'Well!' she said, once the girl had finished. 'How very peculiar. My goodness, the others must be furious with me.'

'Of course they aren't, silly,' said Delia. 'They all know quite well that you couldn't help it. It really was queer, Gillian, when you were rummaging about in the common-room in your sleep. You kept saying, "Where is it?", as though you were looking for something.'

'Did I?' said Gillian, looking very surprised. 'I wonder what it could have been. I have absolutely no recollection at all of sleepwalking, or of taking anyone's things, or of looking for anything! I am glad that the others don't hold it against me. I bet that June and Millicent aren't too pleased that I'm going to be out of action, though.'

'Millicent certainly isn't,' said Delia, pulling a face. 'June seemed to take it quite well, though. She is putting Freddie in your place.'

'Good old Freddie!' said Gillian, pleased. 'Delia, wouldn't it be fun if we could get a place on the coach and go along to cheer the team on? I might not be able to play, but it would be nice to go and watch.'

Delia thought that this was a very good idea indeed, and just the thing to speed up Gillian's recovery. She went straight to June, and put the idea to her.

'Yes, it will be nice if we can take some of the Malory Towers girls along to cheer us on,' said June. 'I have already booked a coach for the team, so I shall see if we can get another one to take the girls who want to come and watch.'

The second half of the term was passing very quickly, and there was only a week left until the tennis tournament, and two weeks until the orchestra competition.

Freddie, determined to do her very best for the school, was working hard at her tennis, and, although Gillian's illness had been a blow, June felt certain that her team would make her proud.

But Millicent was not so confident in her orchestra. She gave Gillian's solo to Fay, one of the second violins, and, although the girl played every note correctly, she lacked Gillian's fire and passion. The same could be said of Pam, who rarely made a mistake, but wasn't a natural musician, as some of the others were.

'Neither of them do my music justice,' thought Millicent, who was beginning to think seriously about pulling out of the competition altogether. The dream that she had had of bringing glory to Malory Towers by winning the competition with a first-class orchestra was beginning to slip away. Many of the top musicians had left, and Millicent was forced to admit that it had been largely her fault. She had driven away Anne, Jessie and Kathy. And if only she had been a little more sensitive and understanding with Gillian, and noticed that the girl wasn't well, she might not have become ill either.

Yes, Millicent was learning some hard lessons in the last few weeks of term. If only she had learned them earlier, how much easier her time at Malory Towers might have been!

A big chance for Delia

The day before the tennis tournament, the heavens opened. Walks and horse-rides were cancelled, tennis and swimming were out of the question, and the girls grew very bored indeed cooped up indoors.

June got permission from Miss Grayling to use the telephone in her study, so that she could speak to the games captain of Summerfield Hall, and, reluctantly, both girls agreed that the tournament must be postponed until the following Saturday.

'The same day as the orchestra competition,' said Gillian, when June made her announcement. 'It's just as well that I'm not playing in either, otherwise I would have to split myself in half.'

Millicent was not at all pleased about this, and felt as if June was trying to steal her thunder. She could just picture the tennis team returning home triumphant next weekend, while the orchestra came home dispirited and empty-handed.

June, seeing the girl's sour expression, and correctly guessing her thoughts, laughed and said, 'Don't blame me, Millicent. You can hardly hold me responsible for the rain, you know!'

Fortunately the rain cleared a couple of days later, and the girls were able to resume the outdoor activities they loved so much. Gillian, although she was no longer involved, went along to watch some of the tennis practices, and was pleased to see that Freddie was on top form.

'It makes me feel better about letting you down,' she said to June.

'You didn't let me down,' said June, with her usual frankness. 'I let *you* down, Gillian, for I knew that you were working too hard, yet I let you carry on pushing yourself because I so badly wanted you for the team.'

'Well, I'm enjoying taking things easy now,' said Gillian. 'Delia is making sure that I don't overdo it.'

Delia was, though she raised no objection when Gillian asked Millicent if she could sit in on the rehearsal the following day.

'Of course,' said Millicent. 'I only wish that you were playing, for Fay is nowhere near as good as you.' Then she added hastily, 'Not that I am trying to persuade you to take her place, for I know that you have been ordered to rest. And I don't want Matron after me.'

Listening to Fay play her solo, Gillian had to agree with Millicent. Somehow the whole orchestra seemed listless and lacklustre, the girl thought. They needed something to lift and inspire them.

Evidently Millicent thought so too, for, as the orchestra took a break, she sat down beside Gillian and said despondently, 'We don't have a hope of winning at this rate.'

A sudden thought struck Gillian, and she clutched Millicent's arm, saying excitedly, 'Millicent! Is there anything in the competition rules that says you can't have a singer in your orchestra?'

'I don't think so,' said Millicent. 'Why?'

'I have an idea,' said Gillian, leaping to her feet. 'I'll be back in a minute.'

And, leaving a puzzled Millicent to stare after her, Gillian went off in search of Delia.

She found the girl in the common-room, and cried, 'Delia, come with me, at once!'

'Come where?' asked Delia, looking a little alarmed.

'To the hall,' answered Gillian, taking her arm. 'You are going to save Millicent's orchestra.'

'Me?' squeaked Delia. 'How?'

'You are going to sing with them,' said Gillian, pulling Delia out of the door.

But Delia came to a dead stop at this, saying, 'No! Gillian, I couldn't possibly. Why, I would be simply terrified!'

'You can,' Gillian told her firmly. 'Think of the honour of the school. Think how proud your father will be. And think how sick your aunt and cousins are going to look when they find out that you *do* have a talent, after all.'

Delia laughed at that, but said, 'It's one thing to sing along when you're playing your violin, Gillian, but quite another to sing in front of a hall full of people. My voice isn't good enough.'

'It is,' insisted Gillian. 'You have a beautiful voice, but, as I have told you before, no confidence. Well, my girl, now is the time to look inside yourself and *find* some confidence. Millicent needs you!'

Millicent looked very surprised when Gillian returned with Delia, and she wasn't very impressed on being told that the girl was going to sing along to the violin solo. Delia was a complete duffer, everyone knew that. And she herself admitted that she had no talent for anything. Still, the rehearsal couldn't get much worse, so Millicent allowed Gillian to have her way, and a very scared Delia took to the stage.

She was so nervous that her knees shook as she took her place beside Fay. But then the opening bars of the violin solo started, and something strange happened. The music seemed to take her over completely, so that Delia forgot about Millicent, Gillian and the rest of the orchestra. And as she opened her mouth and began to sing, Millicent gave a gasp.

Delia most certainly *did* have a talent! A marvellous talent. The rest of the orchestra listened, spellbound, as Delia's voice filled the room, pure and clear. As for Fay, she seemed inspired, and played as she had never played before. When the song ended, there was silence for a few moments, then thunderous applause broke out, everyone getting to their feet to clap, and those girls who were closest to Delia patting her on the back.

'My word!' cried Millicent. 'You are a dark horse, Delia. That was simply beautiful. Fay, you played superbly as well.'

'That's because Delia's song somehow brought the music to life for me,' said Fay, grinning with pleasure.

'That settles it, then,' said Millicent, firmly. 'Delia, you must sing with us at the competition.'

The orchestra, along with Gillian, agreed vociferously with this and Delia, overwhelmed and delighted at being the centre of attention, found herself agreeing. Certainly her sweet, simple song seemed to have breathed new life into the orchestra, for the rest of the rehearsal went swimmingly.

Afterwards, in the common-room, Gillian couldn't wait to tell everyone the news, and Delia was persuaded to sing her song again for the fifth formers. They listened, enthralled, then, for the second time that day, Delia was on the receiving end of a round of rapturous applause.

'Absolutely marvellous!'

'You'll bring the house down at the competition!'

'My goodness, Delia, have you any other hidden talents we ought to know about?'

'That's the song I heard you sing once before,' said Felicity. 'You told me that you had heard it on the radio.'

'Well, that wasn't quite true,' said Delia, flushing a little. 'I wrote the words myself, and set them to Millicent's music.' The girl turned to Millicent. 'In fact, I began writing them at that first rehearsal, when I was supposed to be making notes for you.'

'And I was so angry with you,' said Millicent, with a groan. 'Heavens, if only I had known the way things were going to turn out, I would have encouraged you, instead of ticking you off. I always wondered why there was a page missing from the back of my old notebook, and now I know why!'

Delia gave a self-conscious little laugh, and said, 'You'll never know the trouble I went to, to get hold of that notebook, Millicent. I was so afraid that you would read my words and make fun of them.'

Millicent turned red at this, feeling a little ashamed, for she probably *would* have made fun of Delia. Heavens, what a lot of mistakes she had made this term, and all of them in her dealings with people. Well, she was going to make an effort to be a lot more kind and considerate in future.

'Aha!' cried Julie suddenly. 'That's what you were doing the day Lucy and I caught you looking in Millicent's bag! You were trying to find the notebook!'

'And you must have been looking for it when Amy and I found you going through Millicent's desk,' said Bonnie. 'Well, what a relief to have that cleared up! Of course, I never really thought that you were the thief.'

The fifth formers fell silent all of a sudden, everyone looking at Delia, who had turned rather pale. 'You thought that I was the thief?' she said, in a low voice.

'We did suspect you, yes,' said Pam, deciding that it was best to be honest.

'You must understand how it looked,' said Lucy. 'Things suddenly started going missing around the same time as you started going through Millicent's things.'

'Yes, it did look most suspicious,' put in Amy.

'I suppose it must have,' said Delia. 'I never had the slightest idea that you thought I might be the thief. And all because I didn't want Millicent to find the words that I had written!'

'Well, I forgive you for going through my things,' said Millicent, clapping Delia on the back. 'Everything turned out all right in the end. There was no thief, and I have gained a beautiful song and a marvellous singer for the orchestra. Just out of curiosity, though, where *did* you find that notebook? I had been hunting high and low for it for simply ages, then as soon as I bought a new one it simply appeared on my cabinet.'

'Gillian had it in her bag,' said Delia.

'Did I?' said Gillian, looking most surprised.

'Yes, it fell out that day we were in the tea-shop,' said Delia. 'I suppose you must have taken it one night when you were sleepwalking, and for some reason you hid it in your bag, instead of the cupboard.'

'Wait, I remember now!' exclaimed Gillian, clapping a hand to her brow. 'I slipped it into my bag in French, Millicent, the day you got into a row with Mam'zelle. I thought that if she spotted it on your desk you would have got into even more trouble, so I hid it, meaning to give it back to you later. Then I simply forgot that I had it!'

'I thought I was supposed to be the scatterbrain of the fifth form!' laughed Nora.

'Well, we certainly seem to be clearing up a few mysteries lately,' said June. 'The thief that never was, the disappearing notebook and Delia's hidden talent!'

Everyone laughed at that, and Millicent said, 'I, for one, am very glad that Delia's hidden talent has been discovered. She has certainly given the orchestra a new lease of life.'

June looked slyly at Millicent, then she turned to Delia and said smoothly, 'I say, Delia, I don't suppose you're secretly a marvellous tennis player, are you? Now that Freddie's on the team I could do with another reserve.'

Outraged, Millicent glared at June. Then she saw the twinkle in the girl's eyes and burst out laughing.

June laughed too, then she held out her hand and said, 'You and I have had our differences this term, Millicent, but I wish you the best of luck in the competition on Saturday. It will be too marvellous for words if you win it for Malory Towers.'

'And I hope that your team wins the tennis tournament,' said Millicent warmly, taking June's hand. 'My goodness, wouldn't it be wonderful if we both came back to school victorious?'

But when Saturday came, Millicent's victory looked in doubt. In fact, it seemed as if she and her orchestra would not be able to enter the competition at all!

The tennis team were standing in the driveway, waiting for the coaches that would take them and the spectators to Summerfield Hall. The players looked very smart indeed in their spotless white dresses, and when the orchestra came out, wearing their summer uniforms, June exclaimed, 'Gosh, I wish Miss Grayling could see us now! Don't we all look neat and tidy!'

Miss Grayling did see the girls, for she came out to offer a few words of encouragement, accompanied by Miss James and Mam'zelle Dupont.

'I shall be very proud of you all if you win,' she said, with her lovely smile. 'But I shall still be proud of you if you lose, for I know that you will do your very best, and that is what is important.'

'Ah, yes,' said Mam'zelle, beaming at the assembled girls. 'And how smart you all look, is it not so, Miss James?'

'Yes, indeed,' said Miss James, with a smile. 'And now I see that your coaches are coming, so we will leave you to it. Good luck, everyone!'

As the three mistresses made their way back inside, Millicent suddenly gave a groan and cried, 'Oh my gosh!'

'What is it?' said Gillian, looking at her in alarm, for the girl was as white as a sheet.

'Oh, Millicent, don't say that you are ill! How is the orchestra to manage without a conductor?'

'I'm not ill,' said Millicent in a queer, tight little voice. 'I've just realised that I have forgotten to book a coach for the orchestra.'

'Millicent, please tell me that you are joking,' said Pam, dismayed. 'How on earth could you have forgotten something as important as that?'

'I was so wrapped up in rehearsing, and getting the music right, that it went completely out of my head,' said the girl in a hollow tone. 'Well, that's it, I'm afraid. We can't enter the competition and that's all there is to it.'

Millicent could almost feel the wave of disappointment that washed over the girls. She felt bitterly disappointed too, and very angry with herself. How *could* she have been so stupid?

But June, who had overheard, said, 'Wait a minute! Millicent, we have two coaches – one for the team and one for the girls who were coming to watch. It means that we will have to leave the spectators behind, but why don't you take our second coach?'

'June, would you really do that for us?' said Millicent, hardly daring to believe that she had heard the girl correctly.

'Yes,' said June. 'Your competition is in the next town to our tennis tournament, so the driver will only have to go a little farther. Now buck up, and get your instruments on board.'

The girls who had been hoping to watch the tennis were disappointed at having their day out spoiled, of course, but they took it well, and stood aside to let the orchestra get on. Gillian was going with them, for Delia felt quite sick with nerves and had insisted that she would not be able to perform unless her friend came along too.

'I felt quite relieved when Millicent said that she hadn't booked the coach,' Delia confided to Gillian, as they took their seats. 'For it meant that I wouldn't have to sing. Now I feel sick again.'

'You'll be fine,' said Gillian, giving her arm a squeeze. 'I mean to try and get a seat in the front row when the competition starts, so if your nerves get the better of you, you can look at me, and pretend that you are singing just for me.'

But the big town hall where the competition was taking place was packed, and Gillian had to settle for a seat near the back.

'Oh dear,' she thought. 'I do hope that Delia will be all right.'

Of course, Delia wasn't the only member of the orchestra who felt nervous, for several of them could almost hear their knees knocking as they waited backstage for their turn to come. Millicent too was very anxious, but she hid it well, knowing that it was her job to try and have a calming influence on the others.

The competition began, and Gillian, in the audience, watched as one orchestra after another performed. Some of them were very good indeed, some not so good. But none of them had a singer, and Gillian felt sure that, if her friend could only hold her nerve, her voice would win the competition for Malory Towers.

At last it was their turn, and Gillian felt her heart beat a little faster as Millicent led the girls on to the stage. Each girl carried one of the colourful little pennants that Bonnie had made, and as they took their places they hung them from the music stands.

Then the performance began, and it went very well indeed, the audience enjoying it enormously. Then came the violin solo and Delia, who had been standing in the shadows, walked to the front of the stage. She glanced swiftly along the front row for a glimpse of Gillian, but, of course, she couldn't see her. As luck would have it, though, there was a man in the front row who looked very like her own, dear father, and Delia decided that, if her nerves overcame her, she would pretend to be singing for him.

But, once again, as soon as she began to sing, the sick, fluttery feeling in her stomach vanished, and Delia gave a marvellous performance. When she had finished, the audience clapped for so long that it was several minutes before the rest of the orchestra could continue playing the rest of the piece. But Millicent didn't mind the hold-up at all, for the spontaneous burst of applause proved just how well Delia had done.

And the whole orchestra received a standing ovation, once they had stopped playing. Gillian, of course, clapped louder than anyone, feeling absolutely delighted, for none of the other orchestras had got one. Malory Towers had won, she was certain of it!

A wonderful end to the term

Meanwhile, things were also going well for the tennis team. The juniors had only lost one of their matches, while Felicity and Susan had scored a comfortable victory over their opponents in the doubles.

Freddie, too, had played her heart out, and the others had cheered until they were hoarse when she narrowly beat her opponent.

'Well done, Freddie!' yelled June, clapping her on the back as she came off the court. 'I doubt if Gillian herself could have played better.'

And now it was the final match, with June playing the captain of Summerfield Hall.

The two were very evenly matched, for although the Summerfield girl was much bigger than June and had a very powerful serve, she was less agile.

The opposing captain won the first set, and June the second. The two girls were equal in the third set, when disaster struck. June, running forward to return her opponent's service, stumbled and fell heavily, twisting her ankle. The Summerfield games mistress dashed on to the court as June gave a little cry of pain, and administered first aid.

'Well, it's certainly not broken,' she said, after gently feeling the ankle. 'Probably just a bad sprain. Hard luck on you, though. I'm afraid that the match will have to be abandoned.'

But June wasn't standing for that!

'No,' she said firmly, getting gingerly to her feet. 'I intend to play on.'

'Well, you've plenty of pluck, I'll say that for you,' said the games mistress. 'Very well, but if that ankle is causing you too much pain, for heaven's sake say so, before you do any more damage!'

June's ankle was very painful indeed, but she was determined to see the match through. And she did, with gritted teeth, but as she could only hobble it was quite impossible for her to return some of her opponent's shots, and she lost.

'Never mind, old thing,' said Felicity, in the changing-room afterwards. 'Miss Grayling will still be proud of you, for you played your very best.'

'The funny thing is that I *don't* mind,' said June, sounding most surprised. 'It really is queer, for you know how I hate to lose at anything. You, Susan and Freddie all played splendidly, and so did the lower school. So in spite of my wretched ankle, we have won the tournament and that seems to be all that matters.'

'June, I do believe that you've found that team spirit we knew was hiding inside you somewhere!' said Susan.

'Do you know, I think you're right!' said June, much struck. 'Fancy that! Although I suppose, as I'm games captain, team spirit is quite a good thing to have.'

'I would say it was essential,' said Felicity. 'Now come along, for we have to be presented with the cup, then we had better get you back to Malory Towers so that Matron can take a look at your ankle and bandage it up.'

The kitchen staff at Malory Towers, aware that today was a very special occasion, had prepared an extra-delicious tea. Julie and Lucy, walking past the dining-room, glanced in, their eyes lighting up as they saw all the good things being laid out by the staff.

'Fruit cake, chocolate cake, sandwiches of every kind – and my goodness, those scones look delicious,' said Julie.

'Well, I daresay that both the tennis team and the orchestra will be jolly hungry when they arrive back,' said Lucy. 'I do hope that they have good news and this turns out to be a celebration tea.'

The tennis team arrived back first, June and Freddie holding the cup aloft between them, and a rousing cheer went up as they entered the common-room.

'Jolly good show!' cried Nora. 'Do sit down and tell us all about it.'

The two girls were glad to put the big cup down on the table, for it was very heavy, and June hobbled towards the nearest armchair.

'What on earth has happened to you, June?' asked Bonnie.

'Sprained my ankle,' said June, with a grimace. 'I suppose I should go and see Matron, but let us tell you all about the tennis tournament first.'

Matron, however, had other ideas, and a few minutes later she appeared in the doorway of the common-room, saying in her brisk way, 'June, I hear that you've hurt your ankle. Come with me at once, please.'

'Bad news travels fast,' said Felicity. 'How did you hear about it, Matron?'

'The games mistress at Summerfield telephoned to tell Miss Grayling about it,' answered Matron. 'She thought you might need a bandage, and from the looks of it she was right, for your ankle is swelling already.'

'But, Matron, I was just about to tell the girls about our marvellous victory,' protested June.

'Ah yes, I heard that you had won the tournament as well,' said Matron, her face creasing into a smile as she looked at the big cup standing on the table. 'Congratulations!'

'Thank you,' said June. 'Matron, I'll be along in ten minutes or so, when I've had a chat with the others.'

'You will come now,' said Matron, in a tone that warned June she would be unwise to argue. 'You might be a fifth former, but when it comes to your health I still know best.'

Grumbling a little, June limped along behind Matron, leaving Felicity, Susan and Freddie to tell the fifth formers all about the tennis tournament. Matron did her work very thoroughly indeed, and by the time June got back to the common-room, the orchestra had returned.

Another cup stood next to the one that the tennis team had won, and the beaming smiles on the faces of

Millicent, Gillian, Delia and Pam told their own story.

'Everyone played splendidly,' Millicent was saying, as June walked in. 'And as for Delia, she sang magnificently.'

'A double celebration!' said June, patting Millicent on the back. 'How marvellous!'

Just then the bell went for tea, and, as the girls made their way downstairs, Gillian said to Delia, 'I'm awfully proud of you, you know.'

'Thanks,' said Delia, turning pink. 'I'm rather proud of you, too.'

'Me?' said Gillian, with a laugh. 'But I haven't done anything!'

'Oh yes, you have,' said Delia. 'For one thing, you gave me the confidence to sing in front of people. And I really think that you have been an absolute brick today. You should have been taking part in the tennis *and* the competition, and you ended up doing neither. But you haven't complained once.'

'Well, I'm not all that sorry, to be honest,' said Gillian. 'I was thinking the other day, you see, about my sleepwalking. Do you remember telling me that I was saying, "Where is it?"'

Delia nodded, and Gillian went on, 'Well, I think that what I was searching for was my sense of fun. As soon as I started practising in earnest, all of the fun went out of tennis and music for me, and they became a chore. I shall never let that happen again.'

And Gillian never did. As the term drew to a close,

she occasionally partnered one of the others at tennis, or played a dance tune on her violin in the common-room, but only for amusement.

Millicent, too, seemed like a different person now that the competition was over. The girl was much less intense, and joined in the others' fun and conversations without looking as if her mind was elsewhere.

'My music will always be important to me,' she said one day, when Nora commented on this. 'But I'm going to make time for other things too. I'm going to try and have a break from it until I go back to the academy next term.'

'Oh, are you leaving us?' said Felicity, surprised.

'Yes, I only found out myself this morning,' said Millicent. 'My father is going back to work in France, so Mother and I are going with him, and I shall be going back to the academy.'

'We shall miss you,' said Pam, who liked this new, carefree Millicent much better than the old one.

'Well, I shall miss all of you,' said Millicent, genuine regret in her tone. 'And dear old Malory Towers. I have learned a lot here, mostly about myself.'

'Yes, not all of the lessons Malory Towers has to teach can be learned in the classroom,' said Susan.

'My goodness, you do sound wise and learned,' said June. 'Just as a fifth former should. Though I must say, it's about time.'

Unfortunately, Susan then ruined the effect by throwing a cushion at June, who promptly threw it back, only to hit Bonnie instead. She retaliated at once, and soon most of the form was involved in a very undignified cushion fight.

No one heard the door open, or saw Miss James peep in. The mistress retreated at once, extremely startled. Well, really! The fifth formers were always so good and well-behaved in class, and always set such a good example to the younger ones. Who would have guessed that they chose to spend their free time in such an unseemly manner?

But Miss James's lips twitched as she walked away. They might be near the top of the school, but they were still young girls after all, and entitled to let off a little steam.

At last it was the last day of term, and as the fifth formers packed, Delia was called to Miss Grayling's office.

The others were a little concerned, Gillian in particular looking very anxious and pacing up and down the dormitory.

'I say, Gillian, you'll wear the carpet out if you keep doing that,' said Freddie. 'Do calm down. I'm sure it can't be bad news for Delia.'

It wasn't, for the girl looked the picture of happiness when she returned to the dormitory.

'Guess what?' she said excitedly. 'My father is coming home on leave today, for a whole month! He is on his way here now to collect me.'

'That's simply wonderful,' said Pam. 'I'm so pleased for you, Delia.'

'Yes, you won't have to spend all of your hols with

your horrid aunt and cousins now,' said Nora.

'She won't have to spend *any* time with them,' said Gillian happily, giving her friend a hug. 'Delia is coming to stay with us for the rest of the hols.'

'Delia, promise me that you will keep up with your singing when I am gone,' said Millicent, who was busily going round writing down everyone's names and addresses, and making promises to keep in touch.

'I shall,' said Delia. 'It gives me such pleasure.'

'And it gives everyone else pleasure too,' said Felicity. 'What a marvellous gift to have.'

At last the fifth formers were all packed, and they made their way down to the big hall, with their night cases.

'What a racket!' said Bonnie, screwing up her face as they reached the bottom of the stairs.

Indeed it was! Girls yelled, mistresses shouted as they tried to keep order, the parents who had arrived early looked bewildered, and *everyone* kept tripping over the bags and cases that were lying around everywhere.

Mam'zelle Dupont was much in evidence, for she always liked to say goodbye to all the girls, and she beamed when she saw two of her favourites, Nora and Bonnie, coming down the stairs.

'Ah, *mes petites*!' she cried, putting an arm around each of them. 'You have come to say goodbye to your old Mam'zelle. Soon you will be gone from Malory Towers. Soon you will be at home with your loving parents. Soon you will have forgotten all about your school, and the mistresses. Soon –'

'Mam'zelle, we will be back before you know it,' said Nora, a little alarmed. Dear old Mam'zelle took these farewells so very seriously, and at the moment she looked as if she might burst into tears.

Bonnie, noticing that the mistress's eyes looked suspiciously moist, pulled her handkerchief from her pocket, and something else flew out at the same time, landing at Mam'zelle's feet. That wretched brooch!

Mam'zelle, who had a great liking for ornate jewellery, spotted it at once and stooped to pick it up.

'Ah, how exquisite!' she said, holding it in her hand. 'Bonnie, you must take great care of it, for I am sure that it must be a family heirloom.'

'Oh no, just a piece of costume jewellery,' said Bonnie. 'As a matter of fact, I've never worn it, for I don't care for it very much.'

'But it is so pretty!' said Mam'zelle, looking at Bonnie as if she was quite mad. 'How can you dislike it?'

'Just bad taste on my part, I expect,' said Bonnie, her eyes dancing. 'I know, Mam'zelle! Since you like it so much, why don't you keep it? You can wear it in the holidays and it will remind you of us girls.'

Mam'zelle cheered up enormously at this, thanking Bonnie profusely. Then she gave each girl a hug, in turn, before pinning the brooch to her blouse and going off to display it proudly to the other mistresses.

'Well done, Bonnie,' said Nora. 'You managed to stop Mam'zelle from becoming too sentimental.'

'And I got rid of that ugly brooch,' said Bonnie

happily. 'Two birds with one stone.'

Soon most of the girls who were being collected by their parents had gone, and the big hall became emptier, as only the train girls were left.

And at last the big coaches arrived to take them to the station, Felicity and Susan walking down the steps of the school together.

'Another term over,' said Susan. 'And what an eventful term it's been.'

'Hasn't it just!' said Felicity. 'You know, Susan, now I always feel a little more sad at the end of each term than I used to when we were lower down the school. I suppose it's because I know that it won't be so very long before we say goodbye to Malory Towers forever.'

'Well, we still have one more term in the fifth,' said Susan. 'Then a whole year in the sixth, so really we still have quite a time to go. And I intend to make the most of every minute!'

'Yes,' said Felicity, sounding a little more cheerful. 'That's what we'll do, Susan, when we come back. Make the most of every minute.'

Enid Blyton ™

secrets AT
Malory Towers

If you come to the garden shed at 12, everything will be revealed:

- Daffy's latest naughty prank
- What Mam'zelle found in her handbag
- Alice's amazing secret

The sixth form are in for a shock!

There's Mischief AT Malory Towers

Have you read these other great books in the Enid Blyton™ collection?